Thank you for participating

use.

Brandi

Songs of Perdition – Book Two

CD Reiss

Copyright © 2014

This book is protected under the copyright laws of the United States of America. Any reproduction or other unauthorized use of the material or artwork herein is prohibited.

This book is a work of fiction. Any similarities to real places, or persons living or dead is purely coincidental

Cover Art designed by the author

use.

chapter 1.

FIONA

I often drifted off into a trance-like state that reminded me of the hypnosis sessions I used to have with Elliot. I fazed out in the evenings between dinner and lights out while I sat in front of the TV, watching the ocean waves on a loop, and I let my mind do whatever it wanted.

While I thought about nothing, in a cotton-candy medicated haze, the cardboard cone of my rage was hidden under the pink tufts of sugar. In the ten days since Elliot left, they'd changed my meds and I'd run the gamut from zoned out to acting out.

Too much slap, not enough tickle.

I missed Elliot and his cold professionalism, the little tics and movements he used to funnel his emotions, the promise of his naked body under his clothes. He'd been gone twelve hours before I started entertaining vivid sexual fantasies about him. I didn't need him for anything. In the heat of our non-relationship, I didn't need him to set me free or call me sane, so I didn't have to block out the thoughts. Since I'd rediscovered the feel of my fingers on my body, I'd entertained thoughts of him at night once, twice, three times after lights out, falling into a sleepless daze with my hands cupped over my cunt.

My favorite fantasy was so chaste it set my clit on fire.

I'm in a coffee shop on Charleville, the one where I could get a buttercup, which was a drip coffee with butter. I'm alone which, in and of itself, is a fantasy. There are no cameras or paparazzi anywhere. I sit at a table on the sidewalk and open a book. The sun shines. The breeze is light in my hair, and the mug is made of red porcelain.

He stands over me with his paper cup, casting a shadow on my book. "Fiona?"

I look up, and I put him together as I remember him: light brown hair, green/blue/grey eyes, narrow brows, long neck, and a smile that, for once, is genuine, unburdened by self-reproach or professional courtesy.

"Elliot, hi."

"How are you?"

"Great. Do you have time to sit?"

He always sits. Sometimes he's on his way somewhere and decides to take the time out, and sometimes he has nothing to do. But he always sits. I imagine our conversation. I have to make his life up, because I know so little about him. I tell him how well

I am. How I'm cured. How I don't do drugs anymore and how sex is no longer a need. Sometimes I tell him I haven't had sex since I was released, and sometimes I tell him I have, just a couple of times.

When I claim chastity, that's when the fantasy is most vibrant. That's when he walks me to my car and his words of affection, of longing, of repressed desire pulse between my legs. The kiss I imagine, with his hands on my face and his dick pushing against me, makes me so wet I have to rub it off in my mental ward cot.

I imagine going down to Compton, to some rat-infested shelter or run-down church, and seeing him. Our hurt for each other is so strong that the magnetic pull makes our will to remain professional and proper impossible.

He says, "I always wanted you."

I replayed our short time together, looking for moments when that might have been true. As the days wore on, I imagined he has me on the bed. He takes my ankles and spreads my legs so far, and looks at my wet cunt for a second before kissing it. The look on his face is one of bliss, as if he'd been starving and imprisoned and I was a great meal of freedom. When he fucked me, he did it like in the movies, with his face close to mine, eyes half closed, breathing my name.

I knew it was fantasy and impossible. I didn't know the man at all, yet I did. He was normal, straight-laced, probably vanilla. He'd never be with a fuck-up sex addict, a druggie slave worthless whore camera-magnet like me. I'd never attract a man who was plain nice. I didn't have access to the ordinary world, yet I craved it. My darkest desires were for an inaccessible normality.

I hadn't wanted that until Elliot left. In the days following, as my fantasies became more outrageously mild, I thought of Deacon, my master, the one who had helped me function and who I had betrayed. Maybe one day I'd remember the sticky web of circumstances that put us both in the stables, but did it matter a fuck? In the end, did I stab him to be free of him?

And free to do what?

Fuck? Snort? Party?

Or free to be normal?

chapter 2.

ELLIOT

I didn't like rushing. If everything was done properly and in the right order, I never had to rush. Even the most tedious parts of the day could be managed effortlessly if they happened when they were supposed to.

On Tuesdays, I had therapy before work. As a therapist, I needed my own therapy sessions in order to maintain my sanity, though some weeks I had nothing to discuss and my sanity was only impaired by having to spend yet another fifty minutes in Lee's office, talking about nothing. Those sessions supposedly gave me an angle from which to see the seemingly unproductive sessions with my own patients, but I felt more and more like I was wasting my time.

I opened my car door. The bougainvillea that hung over the driveway needed a trim. I often did the trimming myself because I found it soothing, but since

I took the job at Westonwood, I had stopped. Since the gardeners had been instructed to leave it alone, they did, and it exploded into a waterfall of purple blooms that dropped onto my windshield.

I'd gone back to work at the Alondra Avenue Family Clinic in Compton. I'd left a chaplaincy there that had had a limited time frame. They'd asked me to stay on, but I went to Westonwood. When I left the enclave for the rich and troubled, I picked up some part-time work at Alondra while I sorted out my life. I didn't like the instability any more than I liked the upset schedule, but I needed the balance badly.

L.A. traffic was famously brutal, but it was easily managed if one took into consideration the season as it related to the LAUSD, the time of day, the weather, and were willing to change routes at a moment's notice. If I turned right on LaCienega at 7:01 a.m. on a normal Tuesday, I'd be on time. Turning at 7:02 made me upward of ten minutes late. I never figured out where the eight minutes went, but that extra sixty seconds seemed to increase the density of the traffic arteries by an order of magnitude.

So when I turned at 7:04, I assumed I'd have to apologize as soon as I walked into my session. That always led to an explanation of why I was late, and why it was important to be punctual, and back to how I felt about it, and so began the digging like kids in the yard, looking for treasure that wasn't there. But I'd forgotten that it was still Christmas break for the LAUSD, and the roads were clearish. I pulled into the alley behind Lee's office and took a deep breath. I'd made it, and I'd get to Alondra in time because the traffic was light. Being late for Lee was forgivable. Being late for my patients was egregious. They were people who had nothing reliable in their lives but me.

"Why do you worry about them?" asked Lee, her fingers laced together over her pregnant belly. She'd managed to get knocked up at forty-two, and I often found her in a state of bliss, sickness, or a meld of the two.

"Because I'm human. It's human to care."

"But it's not your job."

We'd had that discussion a hundred times. My job was to give patients a safe place to work on their problems. If I cared about them, I'd be emotionally shredded at the end of the week/month/year, and unable to work with the rest.

I didn't answer her. There was no point. I felt fidgety and caught myself rubbing my upper lip with my middle finger. I had nowhere to put the energy. I'd been that way since I left Westonwood.

"You were almost late this morning. I saw you pull in." Lee indicated the window beside her desk, looking onto the parking spaces. She didn't have any tics. World's perfect therapist, recommended by my mentor for her completely calm, organized, non-distracting demeanor.

"Jana caught me in the shower," I said, remembering the perfectly pleasant, if ill-timed lovemaking in the bathroom. "Set my morning back." She'd moved in six months before, after a whirlwind of dating, and had made little or no impression on the house except to be the prettiest thing that had ever stepped foot in the kitchen.

"Ah," she said. "Can I assume things are going well?"

"The usual. She wants me somewhere safe. She thinks I'm going to get jacked every day. She puts on a show of panic and worry. I soothe her. It works for a little while, et cetera et cetera…"

"And she wants you back at Westonwood."

"Yes."

"Did you tell her why you left?"

That was sticky, very sticky. Only Lee was qualified to unravel it, and she was the only person I'd trust with that level of complexity. I'd downloaded my desire to protect Fiona from her family and the media to her during the fist session after I left Westonwood, and she'd let me dance around it, waiting for me to describe my exact feelings in my own time.

"Jana wouldn't understand," I said.

"You should try."

"She's a delicate person. If I tell her about a patient's family pressuring me, she'll worry. If I tell her about the countertransference, it's worse."

"Countertransference happens. The thing with the girl's family, that's something she deserves to know, and it's well outside the privilege of the room."

"There's nothing to tell," I said. "That's what I told you—it was all inference. If I express inference, she's not going to have a place to put it, so it goes in the panic bucket. She can't deal with things that aren't facts."

"How are you going to live like that, Elliot?"

"You make my eyeballs ache, you know that?"

"You've said the same about Jana."

I sneered, knowing it was a sneer and she'd think it was funny. She was pointing out my transference, the redirection of feelings related to someone outside the room to the therapist. Transference was necessary. Countertransference, where the therapist placed unresolved feelings onto the patient, was trickier. Though it was normal, my countertransference with Fiona had to be dealt with. That was why we needed therapy for the therapy, to keep things in check.

"I didn't trust her father's motives," I said. "He comes in and tells me I should let her go. Tells me they'll take her in and watch her and thanks me very much for my time. The way he said it, it was off."

"So you think he should have asked you to keep her for more observation?"

"I think the fact that he even asked is a problem. If he'd asked me to feed her at noon, I would have fed her at eleven because I don't trust him."

"That's very reactionary," Lee said.

"You've never met the guy."

"And do you consider your decision meddling?"

"Anyone with a television knows what's going on. The media frenzy around her brother's accident and her stabbing her boyfriend; no sane person could survive it. She'd go back to using. Letting her out would have been setting her up for failure."

She leaned back in her chair. I didn't know if she needed the belly space or if she was taken aback by my tone.

"You believe that you made this decision based solely on the data?" she asked.

"Lee, what's the difference if it was the right decision?"

"You tell me."

I didn't, because I wasn't ready to say out loud that I had feelings for Fiona Drazen.

chapter 3.

FIONA

I didn't require black dark to sleep, which was good since I fucked anywhere, any time, and sometimes I needed to drop off afterward. Once I woke up on top of Owen Branch on the floor of Club Permission Granted at ten thirty in the morning. All the lights were on, and ladies in blue smocks were vacuuming to the Spanish music on the boombox. Owen wasn't even fully awake when he lit a doob and handed it to me. I went back to sleep for another half an hour.

But at Westonwood, I had a problem I'd never had before: Everything kept me up. I knew I couldn't blame it on the light coming through the door window, or the crickets, or the whooshing of the pipes whenever someone, somewhere flushed.

It was stabbing Deacon and the waterfall of guilt that followed. Everything I'd done in my young life. Everyone heartbreak. Every careless betrayal.

Every time I hurt someone to fulfill some minor need or wisp of a desire. For ditching Owen the morning after the high school prom. For sucking his dick the next week because it happened to be there. For throwing his phone out my car window on the 101 when he told me he'd snuck a shot of my mouth on his cock because it was such a pretty sight. For pulling the car over and punching him in the face, then telling everyone what he'd done until no one would hang out with him any more.

People in my position—meaning people other people looked at—didn't like Sneaky Petes taping fuck sessions, even if they told me nicely what they did and only did it for themselves. No. Just no. That was why phones were surrendered at Deacon's place.

But still. I wasn't focused on my rightness. My rightness didn't hurt, and I was after full-bore self-immolation. So I did what I did every night at Westonwood: I chose a random incident from my life and turned it over in the dark. That night it was Owen. I didn't have to punch him in the face. He'd been a harmless surfer with a huge dick and a permanent boner. I didn't have to make sure none of my friends spoke to him again, or throw his phone out the window on the freeway. It was expensive to him, and I hadn't given a fuck.

Somewhere, a toilet flushed. The pipes whooshed.

It was morning.

***

I didn't tell my new therapist shit. She was just a bitch behind a desk who pretended to support my "healing process." The fact that I'd never put my fist in her face was a testament to my healing process, but I walked out of there twisted in knots every time. I was sure she and the fistful of drugs they gave me were the source of my insomnia. I hadn't slept more than a couple of hours a night since Elliot left.

"You're not schizophrenic," my new doctor bitch said. "You don't suffer from narcissistic personality disorder. You have no history of compulsion."

Her office was a museum of Native American artifacts. Dream-catchers. Masks. Beaded wall hangings and handmade blankets in frames.

"You're saying there's nothing wrong with me." I wasn't even hopeful, just killing time. We'd had that conversation a hundred times already. I didn't know what she was waiting for me to realize, because I'd have the epiphany of the century if I knew.

"The whole idea of sex addiction is a way to impose cultural models to make normal people seem abnormal. Mostly, these normal people are women. If you're not upset with your behavior, then there's nothing to say what you're doing is wrong."

"Then you're going to let me go?"

"What I'm trying not to do it pathologize your sexuality, but your mind is still not clear. Your memory is garbled, and I suspect you went through more in those stables than you're ready to admit.

You're still prone to violence, mostly when men are in the room. I'd like to get to the bottom of it."

Considering I usually lost my shit in the cafeteria at about three o'clock, she was right. It was a co-ed facility, so there were always men around. The only time men weren't around was in that room with her.

"Do I need to be here for you to do that?" I asked. "Because you know, we're supposed get me back to functioning in society. This isn't a whole thing where I'm walking out some healed person who can get a job and land a good husband, right?"

"You're here. This time is for you. Think about it. I could buy you enough time to really get to the bottom of your issues with Deacon and your father."

She presented it like a birthday cake. The luxury of the century. An indefinite amount of time at Westonwood Spa, with the mental equivalent of hot rocks and exfoliating rubs, with her inferences about my father, who I hadn't mentioned to her, and Deacon, who was none of her business.

"And you walk out with what?" I said.

"I don't understand your meaning." She tilted her head, her pin-straight Brazilian blowout falling perpendicular to the earth while her face rested at the angle of inquisitiveness.

"I mean, we find some deep trauma in like, what two, three months, and you? It's a lot of work for you."

"It's work I love. Helping you to heal yourself," she said.

"Don't you have some high-paying gig in Beverly Hills?"

"I have a private practice, yes. Where are you going with this, Fiona? Are you afraid I'll abandon you like your last therapist?"

She should have known better. I'd cut her off the last time she'd tried to come down on Elliot for leaving, because I figured out that when he'd admitted to leaving to protect me, he'd only admitted it to me. I wouldn't betray him, and more than that, I respected him. But there she was, with her patronizing little smile and her forearms on the desk, accusing Elliot of shit outside her sphere of fucking knowledge.

I hated her. Maybe I hated her because she wasn't Elliot. Or maybe I hated her because I didn't want to be there. Maybe I just hated her because she was hateful, and because she was trying to get me to hate men instead of her Brazilian blowout.

And fuck, I hated her Brazilian blowout.

Most of our sessions went like that. I just disagreed with whatever she said. She said the sky was up, and I insisted I walked on clouds. She told me I was sick, and I said I was fine. She'd tried to con me into agreeing that my father had molested me, that Deacon beat me in a way that was non-consensual, that in fucking whomever I wanted, I'd agreed to be degraded. She couldn't get that the fucking itself wasn't degrading. The intentional degradation was degrading. And hot.

I didn't understand her. Why did she seem to care so much? Why couldn't she just listen to my problems, decide whether or not I was sane enough to be questioned, keep my meds low so I didn't feel like throwing things, and let me go? Surely the hospital didn't need my family's money that badly.

"It's not about money," Karen said one day at lunch. She was on a feeding tube and rolled her IV around with her. Mostly she was too weak to even get up, but when she did, she managed to find me. "You're like this rare creature. Rich. Famous. Living in a fish bowl. How many of you are there in the world? And you're in their chair. They can latch on to you and use you."

"For what? It's all confidential, isn't it?"

"Sure. But you know, over drinks? Who knows what they say at parties to get another client. Or to their own therapists. There aren't any secrets. My last guy wrote a paper about anorexia and wealth, and there was a patient in the paper who sounded just like me. My lawyer couldn't do anything."

"Jesus."

"Yeah. I don't tell these fuckers anything anymore. I don't tell anyone anything. Not even my friends."

What had I told Elliot? Anything? Everything? Dr. Brazilian Blowout hadn't gotten much more than evasion, but Elliot had gotten more from me before he split. I trusted him, but should I? I missed my fish-bowl friends who understood what to say when. I trusted them because they lived a shade of my life.

"It's not all like Ojai," I said. "You've been hanging out with the wrong people. Chill with me when you're out. We'll lay back. It's all on the DL."

"Really?"

"Yes." I pushed my food around. What if Elliot told everyone about me? That I was a sex-addict celebutante who didn't know how or why she'd stabbed the only man who loved her?

I didn't care what people thought, but imagining Elliot at a party, casually talking about my problems without mentioning my name, people's eyes going wide as they judged me—the scene I created bothered me. Elliot casually discussing my problems hurt in a way I couldn't even pin down. It was *him,* how *he* felt.

Did he feel nothing?

Was I just a curiosity to him?

Did he leave because he couldn't stand me?

I couldn't tolerate the thought, and I couldn't banish it from my mind. It played on a loop, and with each successive telling, he was more and more dismissive and contemptuous. I gripped my fork so tightly, the edge indented the flesh of my fingers. I pulled it away and looked at the brown-and-purple ridge it created. I ran my thumb over the skin. It was both numb and oversensitive.

"Did you sleep last night?" Karen whispered.

"No. I can't."

"Are they giving you something for it?"

"It's not working. I need Halcion. That's the only one that works."

When someone put their hand on my shoulder, I jumped.

"Sorry," Frances said. "I didn't mean to frighten you."

I hadn't heard her come up behind me. "It's okay." I said it, but I didn't mean it. She dealt with people like me all day. She knew how to approach. But I was so tired I was docile.

"You have visitors."

I didn't know why I thought it might be Deacon. I still held some childish hope that he'd come get me. The thrill of the thought must have been all over my face.

"It's your sisters."

chapter 4.

FIONA

My sisters.

I had six of them, and a brother. So though Frances had said it as if she was talking about a complete set, there was no way all of them had shown up at Westonwood all at once.

Margie got up as I walked out onto the patio, and she hugged me.

"I'm sorry, sweetheart," she said. "I'm sorry I left you." She pushed me away, holding my biceps. "You look good."

"Are you my lawyer again?"

"No. I just came to see you."

"I didn't like that other guy."

"He's very experienced," Theresa said from behind Margie. "He already got you a new judge."

"Jesus, Theresa. Don't sneak up on me like that." I hugged her, and when we separated, she got her hair back into place.

Some girls become stuck-up bitches early in life, and at eighteen, Theresa was just as stuck up as any of them. Always good, always correct. She sat up straight and chewed with her mouth closed, said please and thank you and dressed right for the occasion. It was an accident of her birth, that perfection. None of the rest of us were as pin straight as she was. She wore her little soup of redheaded genes like a tiara. I had no idea why she even showed up to see me. She hated me.

"So?" I said, throwing myself onto the garden bench and spreading my legs in an unladylike fashion. I wanted to throw my whore body in her face, just to make her uncomfortable. "How are you guys?"

"I'm fine," Theresa replied, pressing her knees together. "How are you?"

"Crazy. What do you want?"

"I came checking after you. It's a courtesy."

"Great, I'm having tea with Spence and Chip at three, then a little badminton. Shall you join for a swipe at the shuttlecock?" I tipped my head back toward the field where the croquet and badminton had been set up.

"Oh, Fiona." Margie swung a chair around.

"Small talk is a lubricant, not an insult," Theresa huffed.

"I've never needed lubricant unless I'm getting it in the ass."

I'd aimed to shock her, and I'd done it. Her face, a mask of perfection under her red ponytail, seemed to fall for a second. I thought I'd hit home until she laughed. Then Margie laughed. I felt a swell of pride in pleasing them, even though Theresa was younger and hateful, and I was mad at Margie. It was as if, in that laugh, they accepted me. They didn't, I knew that, but it was my moment.

"Okay, guys. I'm busy finding wholeness," I said. "Seriously. Why didn't you come with Mom and Dad?"

"They're busy," Margie cut in.

"Yeah, more like, Mom hates discomfort, and since she came around here last time asking if Dad ever touched me, I'm thinking I'm not a happy sight for her right now."

"What did you tell her?" Margie's voice was clipped.

I pressed my lips together then puckered them. "He never touched me."

"Is that what you told her, or is that just a fact?" Margie asked.

"Both."

She scanned my face, looking for any other tidbit, like an open pledge I'd betrayed or the slip of an unsavory truth.

"What do you want from me, Margaret?"

"The judge changed. Dad wants you out. Why, is a matter of speculation," she said.

"He wants to divert attention," Theresa said softly, into her hands. "Away from what's happening

with Jonathan. I know him. I know how he thinks."
She held up her hand, but she looked reluctant to open
pledge. As second youngest, she rarely did. There was
a tacit, unspoken courtesy to the elders that they
opened it.

"I swear to god," I said, holding up my hand,
"sixty percent of my brain capacity is taken up by
what's said under pledge and who was under pledge
when it was said. I'm not that bright, guys. Don't fill
up the bucket, or it's gonna spill."

"Pledge open," Theresa said.

"Okay, go."

"Jonathan." All Margie said was our brother's
name, and the beginning of that potentially long
sentence ended in silence. The chatter of birds and
insects in the garden seemed too loud to bear.

"I know there was something with his
girlfriend…" Something about it nagged me, as if I'd
met her or done something I should be ashamed of.

"Rachel. She's dead," Theresa said, closing her
eyes as if gathering strength. Margie put her hand over
Theresa's and let her finish. "Sheila had a party
Christmas night. Rachel and I went two days before to
help her set up. She knew the neighborhood. So, night
of the party, Rachel shows after most of the family
leaves. Jonathan gets drunk and starts acting like an
ass. She takes off in his car and…." She cleared her
throat before continuing. "They found the car, but not
the body."

"I'm sorry," I said.

"Rachel was my friend. She had a tough home life, so she came back to the house with me a lot. Dad, he... Well, she started getting all gifts and wouldn't say from where, and this was a few years ago. So." She cleared her throat again, and her eyes darted over the garden.

"She and Dad, when she was fifteen," Margie cut in with her businesslike tone.

Theresa picked up the thread. "Jon didn't know until a few weeks ago."

"None of us did," Margie said.

"It's the creepiest thing ever," I said. "Seriously, I thought his thing with Mom was like true love that transcended age. I'm a rose-colored dumbfuck."

"You shouldn't use words like that."

"Fuck fuck fuck."

"Can you stop? This doesn't need to be harder." Theresa's face was tense, her fingers clenched into hooks.

Margie glanced at me, her look telling me to shut the fuck up. Delivering bad news was usually Margie's job, but Theresa seemed hell bent on saying hard things, and it appeared Margie was backing her up.

"Okay, go on," I said.

"They haven't told you because they didn't want to upset you."

"They don't want to upset themselves."

"Jon tried to commit suicide," Theresa said.

"What? When?"

"Little less than a week ago." Her voice dropped. "I found him. He took a handful of pills and gave himself a heart attack. It was awful. I mean, really awful. It's going to break Mom."

I looked at Margie. "He's okay?" My brother, the only boy and the youngest of eight, was the scion, the gem, and an arrogant ass I'd never want harmed.

"He's fine. They admitted him here last night. Supposedly Mom is coming this afternoon to tell you, but you know how that goes."

"Here? They admitted him *here*?"

Margie grabbed Theresa's hand, relieving her of the responsibility of speaking. "They don't send you home after a suicide attempt. They have to figure out if you're a risk to yourself. It's like babysitting, only really fucking expensive."

"You don't have to say that word," Theresa whispered. Theresa turned toward the patio.

In the direct light, I saw she had dark circles under her eyes, and renegade hairs had escaped her ponytail. She'd lost her friend, and her brother had almost died. She had a sister in an institution and a father who liked girls slightly younger than her. I realized she was as much of an addict as I was, and refinement was her drug of choice.

"Are you okay, Theresa? You look like hell," I said.

"She was my friend, but she was also a little in love with money, which is probably why she went from Dad to Jon… God, it's even hard to say that."

"Not easy to hear either."

"I think she was trying to blackmail Dad," Theresa said. "It's such a mess. I've never seen Dad like this. He's *afraid*. That's scarier than anything."

"He's not scared," Margie cut in. "He's playing at it. And yes, she was trying to blackmail Dad. I got that through my own channels."

"Why didn't he just pay it?"

"Maybe he did," Margie said. "But she kept coming after him."

"Then me," Theresa said. "She kept saying hateful things to me about Jonathan and Dad, like she was trying to get me to hate them. I was weird about her dating my brother, then I wasn't. Now I am again. But when you see Jonathan, can you tell him I'm sorry? We had this big fight just before. I called him names, which was… I don't know what came over me." Her hands sat palm up in her lap, and she stared at them. "We can't fight amongst ourselves. Reporters are asking questions. It's nuts out there. They're asking about Rachel, about you. They want to use us. Everyone has a camera, and I don't want us to be used any more."

"We're the world's circus," I said. "Third ring to the right. I don't know how to shake it."

"I'm going to." Theresa set her jaw, and a steel curtain dropped over her face. "I'm going to be normal. I'm going to work and have a job like anyone else. I'm going to have friends who like me for me. Not for money or fame or any of this."

"Good luck with that," I said, already shaking my head over her failure to achieve the dream of being no better than ordinary.

On the way out, with Theresa half a hall away, Margie took my hand. "Keep your shit together, and you can get out. Your mandated time is only a few more days, and your boyfriend's not pressing charges, so you can probably avoid a lot of questioning and ugliness if you stay low. But a little sisterly advice."

"As opposed to what you usually give?"

"Jonathan's going to need you. He's not himself. Be there for him. It really is a circus. They've been poking around Dad, which means there are going to be questions."

"I told Mom to talk to Carrie. I'm sorry, I just—"

"It's okay. Forget it."

"Carrie always knew Dad had a thing for... I can't even say it. I always thought she... I can't say that either." I couldn't say that Carrie had always maintained that Dad liked young girls, and that made me think she'd gotten some form of sexual attention none of the rest of us had. I had no proof, just a twist in the gut. Carrie had never said one way or the other.

"Carrie can take care of herself," Margie said. "If I were you, I'd stay in here as long as possible. As a matter of fact, I'd like to admit myself right now."

"If you were in here, I'd work like hell to get you out."

"You're implying... what?"

"You ditched me."

She put her hands on her hips. "For your own good."

"Isn't it about time other people stopped deciding what was for my own good? Maybe treat me like an adult who can make her own decisions? I have my own reason for wanting you to be my lawyer, and it has nothing to do with your experience. I don't want to explain myself to some strange, experienced person. I need someone to work with who I am. Do you get it?"

She didn't answer. She pecked me on the cheek and stalked off for the door. From Margie, that might as well have been a signature on the dotted line.

chapter 5.

FIONA

I'd left my sisters with promises and comfort I was ill-equipped to give. Only someone as naïve as Theresa would tell a psycho like me a thing, and only a Drazen psycho would keep that fucking promise to death.

"They wanted to visit. What's the big deal, Deena?"

Brazilian Blowout's name was Deena. It made me want to kick a puppy.

"You look upset," she said.

"I'm not upset."

"You still have no recollection of what happened the night before you arrived here. Honestly, I find it hard to send you home before you remember."

"It's not a condition of my release. Not according to my lawyer."

"We have some latitude."

"You mean *you* have latitude. You know the violent outbursts were valid. This other bullshit is just bullshit."

"What exactly do you think is going on, Fiona?" She had her forearms on the edge of the desk, and her fucking blowout at a right angle to the earth, and a practiced, blank expression that created a vacuum that sucked the truth out of me.

"I think you're looking to make a career jump." Even as the voice in my head told me to stop, I kept on. "I think you're going to change the names to protect the guilty and write a paper about the famous, debased heiress with a father who married his wife real young. I think you put me back on Paxil, which Elliot took me off of, so I'd have less control over myself and I'd get snappy in the afternoons."

"There's no proof Paxil has that side effect." She sat back, crossing her wrists in her lap. "It's interesting you think Dr. Chapman had your best interests at heart though."

"I think you're vile." I was white hot, and nothing could stop me from burning that shit down. "I think you're a heartless cunt. I'm a *thing* to you. A new trinket on your shelf. You think I'm your fucking gravy train, and I think this hokey Indian crap is all for show unless sleeping with that blanket's going to give me smallpox."

"Let's talk about—"

"Fuck you."

"Your feelings are—"

"Fuck you."

"Fiona, this is—"

"Fuck you."

"Deacon contacted the hospital."

"Fuck you."

"He wanted to see you."

She'd done it. She'd stopped my torrent of hate with a sliver of hope. "This is a trick. I—"

"I told him that until you participated fully in your therapy, he would not be allowed in."

"What?"

"Tell me, Fiona, would you allow him here if you were on this side of the desk? Your last violent episode outside these walls involved him. You've blocked out the memory of it. Seeing him could open floodgates you're not prepared to—"

At the word floodgates, I was finished. Floodgates had opened all right. I remembered it very clearly. The pressure on my right foot as I stood, the pressure of the hard wooden desk on my left knee, the feeling of falling as I straightened my leg on her desk, my thrust forward as I made sure to get my arms out in time to latch my hands around her motherfucking lying throat.

I think I was screaming, which must have been what saved that bitch's life.

chapter 6.

ELLIOT

Like any self-respecting monied hippie from San Francisco, Jana was in therapy. And like any functioning neurotic, she didn't reveal the depths of her neuroses until we were deeply involved.

My father said my time in seminary had made me too concerned, too warm, too compassionate to see what was face value to everyone else, but my father had never been known for his humanity, only his data analysis and domineering attitude. The data told him Jana was beautiful, and his dominance told him she was a handful.

In the sweet opening months of our relationship, while I was doing good work in a chaplaincy at Alondra House in Compton, Jana was my refuge. She didn't want to talk about my work, making my time with her restful. We cooked together, played volleyball on the beach, and sat on my porch and drank beer into the night, watching the West Hollywood partiers traipse up and down the block.

But I couldn't keep work and life separated forever. A mother I'd been treating at Alondra had been pimping out her son for drugs. He was eight. I reported it, and the ensuing threats from her gang were pretty frightening. I understood fear as well as the next person. I understood that no one wanted to put someone they loved in the way of hurt, but I wouldn't let an eight-year-old have sex with men in exchange for his mother's drugs.

Sorry.

That had been six months ago, and though the boy had been taken to foster care, and the gang calmed, Jana still bled fear, and I spent most of my free time torn between a desire to soothe her and a compulsion to run away.

"Good morning," Jana said when I came downstairs. She was dressed in an embroidered jacket and suede skirt she and no one else could pull off. Her light brown hair was pulled back in the front and allowed to drape in the back. She was the assistant head of upper school at a swanky little private school, where self expression was the selling point and rigid academics were the reality.

"Hey," I said, refusing the coffee she handed me. "I'm running late."

The TV was on an entertainment news show. Another Drazen story about Fiona. The same clip we'd all seen a hundred times: her approaching a black Range Rover with her pierced nipples exposed by her unbuttoned shirt. Knowing the story behind the famous shot didn't make it any less compelling when she winked at the cameras before closing the door.

"Uhm," Jana said, snapping my attention from the TV. "I thought you left at eight thirty?"

"I have a working mother who needs to meet at eight, or she loses her job." I shrugged into my jacket. I don't know what satisfaction I got out of being sharp with her.

"Okay, I wanted to tell you we're looking for a school counselor," she said. "Psychological counselor, and I thought..."

I was intimidating her. I knew it from her expression and the way her sentence drifted off. I hated that. I hated thinking she didn't feel as though she could express herself freely because of my reaction. I put my arms around her. "You thought, 'Elliot doesn't have anything steady, so he might like it?'"

"Yeah. I have your resume. I can just shoot it to Mary."

I kissed her, her apple lip balm leaving residue on my mouth. "Sure. Send it."

chapter 7.

FIONA

I wouldn't say I woke. I didn't actually wake up. I more or less flew over the clouds, dipped below, went back above them and in them. The swash of soft white light hit me in the face as I felt the movement of my body, but not a change in my visual field.

Only my pussy grounded me. Somehow, while my senses were dulled, the throb of arousal became a focal point around which everything else swirled. The physical affected the mental, and the pressure between my legs demanded action.

I opened my eyes. The room around my bed was white with microsuede walls. The floor was a warm linoleum without a seam or disturbance. The fiberglass ceiling had three disks of soft lighting, one with a plastic dome around it. A camera for sure. A sparkling clean toilet. The door was closed, sealed, locked, and there was no window in it.

Solitary.

I snaked my right hand under my waistband because I couldn't think until I rubbed out my exploding clit. Once past my Westonwood-approved undergarments, I felt a sting.

I was sore. Very sore. Red, raw, Sunday morning sore. I put the fingers of my left hand to my nose and smelled pussy. Whatever this stupid drug was, I'd been conscious enough to masturbate for however long I'd been in that room, and still I needed it.

I looked at the corners of the bed. Restraints were hanging from the corners, so they had chosen to keep my hands free. They let me beat myself raw. Maybe they even wanted it. Well, I wouldn't give them what they wanted.

I sat up and looked around, but there was nothing else to see. How long had I been in there? No way to know. I didn't have a watch. I would have had to be conscious to take a meal, and I was sure they weren't interested in starving me.

I looked at the camera, waving. "Hey! Hungry."

I wasn't really, but I wanted to get a reaction out of someone, somewhere. I slid off the cot and stepped forward, cringing. It became easy then to figure out how long I'd been in that room. Some time before I got really hungry, and some time after I rubbed my clit so sore I couldn't walk.

I peed in the little bowl and washed my hands in the little white sink. Were they watching? I was sure they were. Lucky for me I didn't care.

"Hey!" I shouted at the camera. "Was that fun? Watching me piss? It hurt too. You know, for once, I wish you'd have tied me down."

I paced the room, thinking that getting tied down had a purpose. This was punishment. I was being punished for trying to choke my therapist. God, I wanted Elliot. I threw myself on the cot, wanting him. All my sexual fantasies of him went out the window. I wanted to sit across his desk and talk, or lie on the couch and listen to him count backward.

Three.

Two.

One.

***

Deacon has tied me and left me longer than usual.

It's an asymmetrical knotting, a demonstration for Martin. I'm in underpants and a tank top, not that both of them haven't seen and done plenty to my body before. Today is strictly clinical. Supposedly.

I face the ceiling. My right knee is tied bent and looped so my knee is connected to my neck. Left leg extended and connected to my left wrist. Right arm behind my back. Ropes around my jaw, holding my mouth open, and my head connected to the suspending rope.

The crotch of my panties has shifted, as they often do, so that air hits between my legs, and I feel the coolness of moisture drying. Deacon's voice becomes a hum. He shows Martin how to knot, his hands touching my skin where the rope dents it, demonstrating the right tightness and the way to handle a sub without hurting her. Martin's hands, careless and dangerous, fix the ropes at my inner thigh. His eyes are on me as if I'm some object, some fuckthing, the thought of it burning like a rage. He wants me today. I feel it in the way his fingers linger on me.

I can't talk or move, and I'm as swelled as I've ever been. I'm deep in subspace, surrendered to my arousal and my master as he uses me like a doll to teach Martin shibari.

Deacon, whose hands I know even if I can't see him, pulls on a rope, and I swing back and forth like a pendulum. I hear Martin leave as, in my mind, the color of my cunt streaks the air in an arc, the shape of heaven. When I wind down to a small slice of a circle, Deacon put his hands on my shoulders and stops me.

"He is not to touch you, ever," he says, running his hands down my prone body. "He has no control. I'm dropping him when I get back." He pulls the rope from my mouth, leaving me with a taste of hemp.

"Yes, Sir."

"You look beautiful."

"I feel… God, I feel everything."

"How are the ropes?"

"Fine, Sir."

He stands between my legs in a button shirt and jeans, looking at the angles of my body. "You're the most perfect model I've ever had." He puts his hands on my stomach and rests them on my breasts. He strokes the points of my nipples, ending in a pinch and a pull on the rings. "Every time I fuck you, I want to possess you. Your pleasure, your pain. Look." He yanks on the nipple rings, and I strain against my bonds. "How sweet to control you with two pieces of metal and some rope. Do you want me to fuck you?"

"Please."

He slides his finger along my slit, the backs of his fingers on my clit. "Open your eyes." He puts two fingers in me, then three, and my eyes flutter open. His hands are instruments of desire. "Look at me."

I do. He's backlit against the window, and his gaze on me is like ten hands. He takes his fingers out of me and licks them then brushes his thumb over my lips.

"Who do you taste?" he whispers, but his voice has the command of a shout.

"I taste us."

He puts four cunt-soaked fingers down my throat, then slides them out and grabs my jaw, pressing my tongue down with his fingertips. He leans over and speaks in my ear, saying the words he always says before he fucks me, sending me to a place where I surrender all anxiety to him.

"Empty your heart, my kitten. Empty your mind. Open your eyes. Who do you see?" His fingers slide out of my mouth and rest on my throat.

"You," I croak.

"Are you empty?"

"I am."

"Release your body to me. I have you."

He pulls out his dick with his other hand and puts it right at my opening.

"I could watch you all day," he says as he slides in. I groan. "And I might."

He pulls his cock out and presses it against me. His grip on my jaw is tight and painful, and when he slaps my breast before yanking on the ring, I feel a surge between my legs. He slaps again, each one a sting of love.

I am outside myself, in pleasure and pain. He is gentle, for Deacon, even when he put his cock so deep in me it hurts. He doesn't move, using the gravity of the suspension to keep the pressure on. He yanks on a rope, then another, until I am upright. He puts his hand back on my mouth and shifts until the whole of my weight is on him. He's in so deep, not moving, not thrusting, just digging.

"I'm staying like this," he says. "Inside you, until I let you come." Drool drips between us, landing on his stomach. "You're a little whore, kitten, but you're my little whore. Do you understand? I own this mouth. I can fuck it with my hand until you drool. I own this ass, and I'll put a hook in it when I like. Your cunt is mine to fuck with anything I want."

I agree in spittle and grunts. I'm so close, but he's moving so little, it could take forever.

He pulls his hand from my mouth and draws it across my cheek, leaving a trail of drying spit. "You're my prized possession." He thrusts get longer and stronger. He puts his nose to mine as I shift further and further from conscious. "Say it."

"I'm yours." He knows something about the surrender of ownership, the delegation of will, turns me on, and the pressure of pleasure is near explosive.

"Again."

"I belong to you." I gasp between every word. He's so strong, so real, and I feel as if I'm made of foam. "May I come, Sir?"

"Say it."

"I would die without you, Deacon."

"Do you want to come?"

"I would die."

I feel him smile against my cheek, and I think of how we'd started and what we became. Back in that blank room, my fingers rolled over my sore, aching clit on the toilet of the solitary room in a mental hospital.

chapter 8.

FIONA

A meal with a little cup of meds came through the flap in the bottom of the door. It was the usual gourmet shit, eaten on the edge of my bed. I took my meds and slid the tray back out. I'd had two meals in that room, one with eggs and another with a sandwich. I'd masturbated twice more, but the last time, I couldn't come because of the pain.

I spent most of the time sitting on the edge of the bed, wondering when they'd let me out. I slept. I thought about my life, everything in it, and all the rotten things I'd done. I'd stolen Amanda's boyfriend in high school, luring him away with the promise and delivery of a blow job. I'd played it off, because who wanted a man who could be taken away so easily? And the time I fucked Kevin Hartneick and made him cry when I didn't want to anymore. Or inviting Gary Adelstein to join Evan Fronet and me in bed, even after

Evan objected. Or my first anal, just before I turned eighteen, when Gary held me down over the kitchen table while he and Evan fucked my ass until I cried like a little bitch.

Afterward, I'd wept on Evan's shoulder, because it had been my fault, hadn't it? I'd hurt his feelings, and I'd wanted that threesome, right? That's what he said when he pushed my mouth onto his cock later that night—that we were even, and I'd gotten the threesome I wanted. If I'd just relaxed, it wouldn't have been painful, and they wouldn't have had to hold me down.

In the white room in Westonwood, there was nothing to distract me. I couldn't even fuck myself. All I could do was stare at that toilet and that little sink and think, *my fucking God, what have I done?* What have I done? What have I done?

When I'd had that hoof knife in my hand, it was the first time in years. I was cleaning Snowcone's sole. It was already pretty clean because Lindsey cared for my horse more than I did, but I got at the loose frog. My hands blistered, and I was crying.

In that room, with nothing but the toilet to tell, I rubbed my hands. There had been blisters. I saw the little rough brown spots where they'd been. I'd been holding that knife that day. Of all the shitty things I'd done, all the backstabbing, heartbreaking, coldhearted shit I'd done, the worst was hurting Deacon.

In that room that had been stripped of everything sensory, I smelled the stables, the manure and dander, the sharp sting of hay. I heard the scrape of the hooves as I cleaned them. Snowcone, so good, so warm, had taken a minute to remember me. I'd been afraid he'd kick me, so I sat where he couldn't reach. The fear was there, right in the rib that always hurt when I thought of how he'd kicked me last time.

I thought over and over about how I'd abandoned him. How intolerant and hateful I was to dump my responsibilities on Lindsay.

I remembered that night. The dark, the crickets, the fear, the anxiety, the self-loathing. I'd been dead sober. And sad because Deacon and I had broken up. The sharp pain in my wrist reminded me of the breakup, and I thought to myself that I deserved it. That pain was mine. I'd brought it on myself. I scraped too hard, thinking about it, and Snowcone let me know I'd ventured into unacceptable territory by shifting in a way that made me jump.

When I did, I noticed someone behind me, and I sat bolt upright.

It was the door of the white room opening, and Frances walking in.

I didn't remember how many days I'd been in there, if I'd been hopped up on meds or if it had been half a day without meds and just me and the boredom. But I felt changed by the white emptiness, sent through some kind of process that had changed me enough to remember what I'd chosen to forget.

Though I knew it was Frances, I was muddled, somehow still in the scene at the stables, and Frances became the person who'd surprised me. As if propelled to act out the memory, I stabbed her twice in the chest with the knife of my imagination.

chapter 9.

ELLIOT

Jana was cutting open a head of broccoli when I got home. I was nine minutes late, and I hadn't called. I only called if I was ten minutes late, and by the time I turned north on LaCienega, I knew I'd make it inside my no-call window.

And I didn't want to talk to anyone.

"Hi," I said, kissing the top of her head. "How was school?"

"Fine. And your day? How was it?"

"Fine," I said. Fine meant I'd only been slightly beaten down by the events at The Alondra Clinic, where my skills were useless against the constant barrage of suffering. Cushy Westonwood, where the psychic pain had a different cause and the same result, was a cakewalk. "How did the testing meeting go?"

"The fourth-grade teachers want more latitude." I flipped through the mail as she spoke. "The parents' association thinks it's a great idea. But when their kids' scores are low and they can't get into middle school, who gets in trouble?" She pointed at herself with the knife.

I still didn't want to talk to her or anyone, but it looked as though it would be an okay evening. "And Mary Queen of Scots? Did you talk to her?"

"No." She chopped broccoli with a slap. Mary was the head of school, and Jana wanted more control over admissions.

"You should talk to her."

"I did. Your Westonwood experience wasn't on your resume."

I hadn't meant that. I meant she should talk to her boss about what she wanted out of her job.

"You must have sent me the old one by accident," she said.

Freud would have said it was no accident. He would have said I'd known damn well the one piece of experience Mary wanted to see wasn't on the resume I told Jana to forward. What did that say about me?

"I thought you had an updated one, sorry."

"I had a thought," she said, sliding the knife over the cutting board. She glanced at me flirtatiously.

"Really?" I pushed her hair from her neck. She had a lovely neck.

"If you went back to St. Paul's, you could reorganize the discernment committee."

"No," I whispered. I didn't want a committee of good Episcopalian laypeople to decide my future. That last step needed to be mine and mine alone.

"If they approve you, you could get ordained. You could have something steady."

"That's not a reason to give your life to God."

She set down her knife, and I felt her jaw tighten against my lips.

"You complain about suffering and God, and then you go to Alondra where there's nothing but suffering," she said. "It's like you're sticking your face in it out of spite."

I pulled away. I wanted to talk about baseball, or the state of the garden, or traffic patterns at rush hour. The last thing I wanted was an exegesis on earthly suffering. "There's suffering everywhere." Fiona, my little countertransference case, flashed on the screen in my mind. Her suffering was nothing like mine, and of a different grade than any I'd seen.

Jana picked up her knife. After tapping it on the cutting board once, as if releasing her negative feelings, she smiled. "Do you want the spicy sauce with the chicken? Or the mustard?"

"Spicy is fine." I headed to the bedroom to change out of my work clothes.

Jana called to me as I walked. "You were late. I was worried."

I pretended not to hear her. I didn't know why I was so grouchy. Traffic. Low blood sugar. Overwhelmed. Late getting home. Jana's dresser drawer was half open, which made me nuts, and the light in the bathroom was on. Normally those things didn't bother me, but that evening, as I took my jacket off, I walked a razor's edge.

The phone rank. It was Frances's extension from Westonwood. She had no reason to call me. I'd taken an indefinite sabbatical, and the paperwork was all in order.

"Dr. Chapman?" she said.

"Hello, Dr. Ramone."

"I'm sorry to bother you."

"It's fine."

"Your patient, Fiona Drazen, says she remembers what happened the day she was brought in."

I wasn't supposed to be moved by curiosity or anything else. A therapist was simply a vessel for what the patient found important. Curiosity made the therapist's desires more important than the patient's, and that wasn't acceptable.

Except damn, I was curious.

"Really?" I said. "That's interesting."

"She'll only tell you though."

I sighed. I didn't mean for it to be audible, because though one might assume it was a sigh of resignation, it was a sigh of relief.

chapter 10.

FIONA

I don't know how long I was in there, but I was peeled off Frances, given a shot of something, and left on the floor. That would've sucked shit out of a dead dog's ass if whatever was in that needle hadn't made me care about exactly nothing. I was high as a kite, living between sleep and wakefulness, completely aware yet unable to control my own thoughts or body. At least the pain of arousal was gone, like a candle snuffed with spit-wet fingers.

Over and over, I went back to the moment I'd attacked Deacon because I'd been frightened. I discovered details, scents, sounds, and I found peace in it. I'd done it as some sort of reaction to the night, not out of anger. Not in some Machiavellian vision of sharp premeditation. It was just some crazy shit where I was startled and stabbed him.

A little voice piped in through the scene. *Who does this? Have you ever heard of this happening before? Why would this make sense?*

But that voice didn't want me to be happy. That voice was my father with his critical disappointment and my sisters with their distaste.

No, fear made the most sense.

"Fiona."

I came around enough to feel the hard floor beneath me, my cheek on cold linoleum.

"Fiona."

That voice again. Soft putty. The thick fat at the top of the cream jar.

"Doctor," I said with a chapped voice.

He crouched beside me with his elbows on his knees, his wrists dangling. "I see your therapy is coming along."

"I've been proactive about my well-being." I don't know how I put the sentence together, but it slid out, and he smiled. "Are you back?"

"It's complicated."

"Be back."

"I'm not coming back unless you play ball."

I got up on an elbow, and the world swam until Elliot looked as if he was doing a sidestroke when he righted me.

"I'll play."

"You're going to need to rest."

"I remember it," I said. "What happened at the stables. I remember the whole thing."

"And? It makes you feel good or bad?"

use.

Therapist to the core. Facts were fine, but feelings ruled.

"Good," I said. "Great even."

"Focus on that for now."

My brain was cloudy, but I was awake enough to be suspicious of what I had been asked to focus on.

chapter 11.

ELLIOT

"This is a mistake," Deena said.

She sat at the round lunch table, a ball of white waxed paper and a half-eaten prosciutto and buratta sandwich in front of her. She'd picked off the arugula.

"You're not getting a response. I don't see the benefit of keeping you on it." I leaned my back on the counter and crossed my arms. The grey room, with its workers' comp poster and featureless cabinets, had been the scene of many a discussion about patients when I worked at Westonwood, and I fell right back into it.

"A real response takes time, not parlor tricks."

She was referring to hypnosis, which wasn't a trick. I didn't need to defend myself against her for another minute, but I had to get through her first. It begged the question of why I was doing it in the first place.

"How long do you think she's going to be here?" I said. "This isn't a long-term facility."

"What do you want out of this, Elliot? Don't you have souls to save?"

Frances burst in carrying a stack of folders. She attacked the refrigerator and grabbed a wrapped burrito from the freezer. "Dr. Chapman, thanks for coming."

"Frances," Deena said, wrapping up the remainder of her sandwich with a loud crackle. "Do you know—"

"I know everything. It's my job." She threw the burrito in the microwave and slammed the door. "What's not my job is getting attacked. So, first. The family wants her out. Why? I don't know. But the pressure's making it hard to run this hospital."

I didn't know why either. Frances set the timer with three loud beeps, and the machine hissed and creaked.

"They want her out to care for her," Deena said.

"Oh, please," I mumbled.

"First they want her in, then they want her out. I've got whiplash already." Frances was in rare form. The pressure was really getting to her. "I'd lock my kids in a box before I let them face that media circus."

"They're oddly unprotective," I said.

"She needs us to protect her," Deena said.

"Not our job," Frances cut in. "My first responsibility is to this facility. If you ask me, they don't want two kids in here at the same time. It looks bad. So that leads us to the second thing. The judge is irrelevant after thirty days. So as much as he wants her here in spite of everything—because he's in the media circus too, and he wants her off his docket—he's got less say once she can put sentences together and not choke random people. Like her therapist."

"Or her brother," I said.

The microwave beeped. Frances opened the door.

"She has a problem with men," Deena exclaimed as if she'd hit gold. "Having him here could unleash a torrent of old feelings."

"The only misandrist in the room is you, Deena," I said.

She stood like a shot, knocking over the chrome-and-plastic chair. "That is—"

"True," I said. "It's—"

Frances slammed the microwave door. "Enough. Just, enough. I have a budget to put together, and I have a major donor's kid in solitary, and I just got attacked by a hundred-ten-pound heiress, and I'm hungry. Dr. Chapman, do you have room in your schedule to finish this? I know you left, but I'm on my knees."

"No, you're not."

"Don't split hairs."

"I want her off the Paxil."

"Frances," Deena said, "please, I can do this."

"Deal," she said to me before turning to Deena. "No, you can't. I'm sorry, but I need this to run smoothly."

"I'll do it," I said without thinking. At the very least, Jana would be happy about my impulsive decision.

"Thank you."

"Can I do the brother then?" Deena asked.

Frances and I spoke together. "No!"

chapter 12.

FIONA

Jonathan was in the rec room playing ping pong with a wall. Between the reddish hair, his height, and his fluid motion, he was hard for me to miss. The ball hit his paddle with a *thup*, then the wall and the table with a *crackcrack*.

He was a grown man. He'd been the baby, the little boy king for as long as I'd known him. But seeing him there, knocking that ball back and forth, with his arms and shoulders broad and built, I realized how much time had gone by. I felt old.

"Hey," I said, sitting on the windowsill next to the table.

The table was bent in the middle like an L, and he was beating the ball against the other side. He moved fast and never even seemed close to missing.

"Hi," he said, eyes on the ball.

"How are you feeling?"

He didn't answer. *thup crackcrack*

"You look good," I said.

"You want something?"

thup crackcrack

"We're imprisoned together. I thought I'd say hello."

"Hello."

He looked like a man, but he was a boy.

thup crackcrack

"Who's your therapist?"

thup crackcrack

"Guy named Rogers."

thup crackcrack thup

"Don't tell him anything."

crackcrack He caught the ball midair. "What?"

"They're out to use us," I said.

"You're nuts, Fee." He knocked the ball against the table and started again. "Nuts, but I never had you for paranoid."

thup crackcrack

"And what happened with you?" I asked. "I mean, Jesus, Jonathan. Were you really trying to end it?"

thup crackcrack

"You muscling in on my therapist's territory?"

"I just don't understand."

thup crackcrack

"You're really bad at this," he said.

"I'm your sister. I want to know."

"It's none of your business."

thup crackcrack

use.

"Was it Dad? Was it that he was with Rachel when she—"

He smacked the ball onto the horizontal surface, sending it flying to the ceiling. "Shut up!"

"Take it easy, Jon."

"Take it easy? Sure, I'll take advice from you. You're a fucking out-of-control druggie party girl doing God knows what. I don't even want to say more because you're my sister, but I read the papers, okay? You disappear for months, show up at Easter, and no one's seen you since. Even the fucking paparazzi can't find you. Then you're arrested, and shit explodes. Now you want to tell me to keep it under control? I don't even want to be seen with you."

"I know what I am, Jon. I know damn well what I am, and I know better than you who to be seen with when, which was why you didn't hear from me for months. Okay? And fuck you too."

"I asked them to keep you away from me," he said, pointing the ping-pong paddle at me. "You get on my last fucking nerve."

He was a boy in a man's body. I knew about plenty of his exploits. He was at least as out of control as I was. I tried to keep myself from reacting strongly, because I knew someone, somewhere was watching closely. I didn't have to break my gaze with my brother to know it. I took a deep breath. He was family, which made us especially prone to poking at our raw places.

"I just got out of solitary," I said, dropping my voice. "I was in for two days, and it felt like a week.

Keep your shit together. In here, losing control has a price. They're paid good money, and they'll do what they want. They will drug you and lock you down. They will restrain you for as long as they want."

It paid to be an older sister, because in his face, I saw that something had gotten through. His arms were still taut and his chin still jutted out, but on some level, he'd accepted the gift I gave him.

"Promise me," I said, holding out my arms. "Promise you'll try to keep it together."

He put his paddle down and accepted my embrace. "I can't believe she's dead. It's my fault. What this family did to her was so wrong. I couldn't live with it. They euthanize animals, and that's what I am."

"Were you driving?"

"I was so drunk, I don't remember."

Then, as if blindsided with a pie to the face in front of a large studio audience, I laughed.

He pulled away. "What? I…"

I just kept laughing. I pointed at myself, then at him. "It's genetic," I squeaked then held out my hands. "Drazen Dementia."

It wasn't funny. Not really. It was very sad, but he got it. Though he didn't laugh as hard as I did, he chuckled and picked up his little white ball.

thup crackcrack

chapter 13.

FIONA

I couldn't believe I was sitting in front of Elliot again. After talking to Jonathan, I'd showered and eaten before my afternoon session, trying not to think my most sexual Elliot thoughts. He'd see them, or I'd slip, and I didn't want him to know.

Some of his things had been removed from the office, but the fixtures and furniture were the same. The lighting was still warm, and he looked exactly the same.

"You need a haircut," I said.

"I'll get right on that."

"I'm glad you're back."

"Well, I'm not fully back. I'm back for you, but I still have duties at my other job," he said.

"I feel special."

"You are special, but it's simply a matter of redressing a wrong. I shouldn't have left things unfinished with you. I should have known better."

"So why did you do it?"

He shifted his pen on his desk three quarters of an inch. "I had pressure in my personal life."

Two words in, I knew he'd prepared his answer very carefully.

"Really? Someone didn't like you working with the rich kids?"

"My girlfriend wants me here."

I tightened when he said he had a girlfriend. Men who dug ditches didn't work harder than I worked to hide the shot of adrenaline that went through my system.

"Okay?" I said. "So you should be here then."

"It would be inappropriate for me to get deeply into it, but I can't do things to please other people. Things came to a head at home just as my recommendation for you was due. The other job came up, I felt I was needed there, and I finished here. But I wasn't. I'm not finished with you at all."

He couldn't have meant it the way it sounded, with his eyes on me as they were. He couldn't have intended to send a stinging rush of fluid between my legs or to set my nipples on end. My throat closed. I had no words, and I always had words. No man in the history of my cunt had ever rendered me speechless.

"I'm told you're not sleeping," he said.

"It's not out of spite."

"Does this happen often? Insomnia?"

I shrugged, looking out the window. The sight of him distracted me. "Sometimes, when Deacon was away. Other times, when there was a lot going on. I get stressed, you know."

"You're on Ambien."

"It's not working. Halcion works."

"It's very habit forming," he said.

"So is talking to you." Talk about habits! Coming on to an attractive man just because I could, even with my little Velcro-closure shoes and V-neck scrubs with no tie at the waistband. I laughed softly in a little huff of breath. I was a mystery even to myself. I needed sleep, and I needed sex. "Deena said Deacon wanted to see me."

"Yes."

"Well?"

"Well, what?"

"Are you letting him come?" I asked.

"I'll meet with him first. Then if I feel that you aren't a danger to each other, and you still want to see him, you can see him."

"I want to see him."

"What do you think he'll say?"

He wanted to know how I felt about Deacon and where we were in our relationship. What he didn't know was that I was so happy about the visit that I didn't care what Deacon would say. I wanted to suck Elliot's cock for just allowing it.

"I think he'll say lots of things."

"Such as?"

I leaned forward, putting my elbows on the desk and the heels of my hands on my cheeks. "He'll tell me I look nice."

"What if he tells you what happened at the stables?"

"I know what happened. I was there scraping Snowcone's hoof. It was late. When he came in, the horse shifted. I had been afraid Snowcone was going to kick me, and I had an adrenaline rush. When I saw a man standing behind me, I went after him with the knife. I guess I freaked out. I mean, stabbing your Dom is not a small deal."

"And you came up with this when?"

"In solitary. I kind of tranced out and remembered."

"You used self hypnosis. That's good, mostly."

I didn't care about the conversation. My body felt aligned with his, poles of energy wanting to attract into a wider, stronger bolt of life. Maybe he felt it and maybe he denied it, but it was there. Sex was my superpower, and I knew when a man wanted me.

"Why mostly?" I ran my fingertip over his desk, considering the ridge between the blotter and the wood with a lazy intensity.

"Mostly, because your memory makes no sense. It has to jibe. I've been startled before, but that goes away in an instant."

"You think I made it up?"

"False memories under hypnosis are pretty common, and they're always in the subject's favor."

Wait, he was implying that the stabbing was premeditated? Was that it? Or was it that I was lying to myself? That the relief I felt was false and based on nothing? Bullshit. I knew that memory was right. *Knew.* The fucker… Was he trying to keep me here, or was he just trying to get some kind of upper hand?

I kept calm and sighed. I pushed a pen a couple of inches before popping it in his cup. He was right across the desk, and I wanted him to take me like his little vanilla whore.

"I think I know what Deacon's going to say," I said.

"Go on."

I leaned forward, my butt barely on the chair, and made my voice milkshake thick. "Kitten, you've been so bad. So very naughty. Do you think I won't punish you? My sweet little slut, you do these things so I'll hurt you. So I'm going to have to now. Let me tell you what we're going to do when you're back. You're going into my office. You're going to bend over the desk, pull your panties down halfway, and spread your legs. There will be a paddle on the desk. You will place it on your lower back. Then you're going to wait. When I come to you, I will take the paddle. You're getting a full twenty strokes on your bottom and the backs of your thighs with it, kitten. Call out the numbers as I do it. You are not to scream. You may spit, you may cry, but you may not shout. You may only thank me. When I've done twenty, you are to take your ass cheeks in your hands and spread yourself for me. Your fingers on your raw skin will burn, but I don't want to hear any complaints. No crying. No blubbering. You may beg me to fuck you. When I believe you mean it, I'll take you. I'll push your face to the desk when I'm fucking your cunt, then your tight little ass. I'll bury myself in you until your skin is too tight to take me, and I want nothing but gratitude when I come on your back, do you understand?"

I watched Elliot's face and saw nothing. Not a blip.

"You must think he's very angry at you."

"That's what he'll say if he's *not* angry. If he's pissed, well, he won't make promises. I know him." I waited for a response and thought I saw a flicker of emotion. I expected disgust, which was how most people reacted to a relationship like Deacon and I shared, but it wasn't that.

"Session over," he said. "See you in the morning."

chapter 14.

ELLIOT

I slammed the door behind me and locked it, fumbling
with my belt and zipper as if I was an adolescent
twisting the last few moves of a Rubik's Cube.

My dick was swollen purple, the skin stretched
over throbbing blood vessels. The pressure on my balls
was enormous, as if a million troops stormed the gate.
I stroked myself over the toilet three times then
exploded, biting back a grunt as I unleashed a torrent
onto the back of the lid. It was more than a release, the
pleasure of it lasting beyond a simple discharge.

My mind wasn't my own. I let it make the
pictures Fiona had called up, her pink ass under my
hands, her cries, her legs restrained by her clothing, her
body stiffening with a wet grunt when she came,
crying my name then whispering it like a prayer.

God help me.

chapter 15.

FIONA

One of the rec rooms overlooked the front of the
grounds. I knew he was coming. I knew Elliot would
call right after the session, and Deacon wouldn't delay
a second to see me. When I saw my master's black
Range Rover come around the front drive and pass into
the parking lot, I felt as if a hundred interlocking
pieces had fallen into place.

I said it, I meant it, things happened as
predicted. That was what it was to have Deacon in my
life.

"Hey, someone here?" Karen was behind me,
toting her IV tower. The sun blasting through the
windows made her look hollow.

I wanted to hold her down and force-feed her a
cupcake. "Deacon."

She stood next to me and peered out the
window. We'd heard much about each other's lives in

the past weeks. I'd have even have called her a friend at that point.

She leaned over beside me. "I can get you Halcion."

"How?" I whispered back.

"Warren's out for his sister's wedding. He's getting me something. I can put in an order for you."

I looked at her skull of a face, blue eyes bulging without flesh to hold them in. She'd been so pretty when I met her.

"What is he getting you?" I asked.

"Something I need and they won't give me."

"Please tell me it's not uppers."

"I have a mother already."

I dropped my voice to barely a whisper. "You don't need diet pills, Karen."

"Do you want the Halcion or not?"

Deacon gave the valet his keys and headed for the door. He buttoned his jacket and walked in that way only Deacon could, a mix of fierce intention and poise, a stew of dignity and ruthlessness.

"He's beautiful," she whispered.

"A thoroughbred."

As if his inner GPS had a little red dot homed in on my location, he looked up at me as he crossed the drive. I put my finger to the glass. He smiled and held up a finger, pressing it against an imaginary glass pane between us. He got closer to the building, and when I could only see the top of his head, he disappeared from sight.

I hadn't realized how anxious I'd been until I couldn't see him. Like the hum of a car engine that didn't bother you until it was gone, the thrum of my heart stopped and the pain disappeared. Karen put her arm around me because I'd put my hand to my mouth to hold back the tears.

"It's okay," she said, not even knowing why I was emotional.

"He's not mad," I said. "He still loves me, and he's not mad."

I would have said that nothing could disrupt his love for me. Not even a hoof knife twice in the chest. But seeing him smile and put up that finger, I realized I'd been crushed with worry. When that worry disappeared, the space it occupied was filled with joy. I hugged Karen, rattling her tubes, and she gave me a rare laugh.

"I'm just…" I started but couldn't finish. "I can actually breathe without pain. I have to get used to it." I threw myself onto the light grey couch.

Karen sat next to me carefully, so as not to disrupt her IV. "You're relieved."

"Yeah. I feel like everything's under control again."

"He did that with a look?"

"That's us."

"Maybe you'll sleep now."

"No. Just have Warren get the pills. I'll pay him when I get out."

Karen waved the idea away. "He doesn't want money. He has plenty. He'll ask for a favor or something. He just wants friends. He's lonely."

"Okay." I craned my neck to watch the valet drive Deacon's car into the lot.

"Aren't you going to run down and see him?" asked Karen.

"Elliot wanted to meet with him first. I guess to make sure he won't upset me. Which, I mean, I know he won't now. So they'll schedule a visiting time and, oh God, this is so great."

I leaned back on the couch, and Karen sat straight up. She looked tired and wrung out. Her battle with food wasn't going well. She said the only time she felt in control was when she wasn't eating. She was defined by her refusal, and when she accepted food, she felt indefinite, sloppy, out of control.

I knew plenty about her life. Before Amanda died, we'd had a lot in common, between the drugs and the sex. Food wasn't what should have made her feel out of control, but who was I to judge?

"I wish I had a Deacon," she said.

"One day, you might."

I felt like the queen of the ball.

chapter 16.

ELLIOT

I had to get to Alondra, but I had to meet Deacon.
Frances had offered to take the meeting, but protocol
be damned, I didn't trust her motives. Mostly though,
after Fiona's monologue about pain and pleasure, I
found myself driven by an unprofessional level of
curiosity again.

He wasn't what I expected.

I'd expected a dirtbag in a wifebeater and
camo. I expected a trashy goatee and a flashy car.
Mostly, I expected to look at him and wonder how he
could make a slave of a woman who could have any
man she wanted.

But he wasn't any of those things. He was
wealthy, obviously. His jacket fit as if it was custom
made, and his hair fell in a conservative drape. His
face hadn't been shaved in a day or so, but it was the
style. He carried himself with assurance. I couldn't see

the valet's position, as he was behind the hedge with someone else, but Deacon seemed to sense his presence. He didn't concern himself with the valet until he was close enough to hand over his keys. Deacon seemed at one with the space around him, at peace and in control.

I knew the patients looked out the east window to see who was visiting, and when he looked and held a finger to the upper floor, I knew he must have seen her. In that gesture, much of my curiosity was sated. Another tangle of emotions took its place.

"Mister Bruce," I introduced myself as he approached reception. "I'm Dr. Chapman."

"Nice to meet you."

We shook hands. He looked me in the eye. Two gentlemen trying to protect the same woman, probably from each other.

I led him to my office and showed him the chair in front of my desk. In a last millisecond decision, I didn't sit behind the desk but in the chair next to his.

"I notice an accent," I said.

"I'm Afrikaner. From the south." He said it with a thick Dutch accent. I could almost hear the k. "I grew up on a farm about two hundred clicks outside Queenstown."

"I've never been."

"To Queenstown?"

"To Africa."

He smirked, and I felt like an ignorant American.

"How long have you been in Los Angeles?" I asked.

"A few years. Business takes me back every few months, to the DRC mostly. Not home."

"May I ask your business?"

"I run a photography agency. Photojournalists working in risky assignments. We hire photographers, buy ransom insurance, track them down if they don't check in, liaison with embassies, negotiate terms of release, this sort of thing."

"Terms of release?"

"When they're kidnapped. The authorities are as useless there as anywhere else." He said it with cold aplomb, as if reminding me of something I had forgotten.

"Ah," I said. It wasn't a question, but an opening for more. It was a hole in which the other person was supposed to pour information, and it usually worked.

In the case of Deacon Bruce, something else happened. "How is she?"

"Without betraying a confidence, she's better. She came in confused. She's gotten her bearings, and she's managing. She's still struggling with her memory of what happened that night."

He nodded.

"I assume you remember?" I asked.

"I tripped and fell."

"You always so clumsy?"

"I get my coordination from my mother's side. Dutch, you know?" He smiled ruefully, and I knew I wouldn't get anywhere with him. "I'm concerned about Fiona. She's not violent. Fiesty, sure. And strong. Very strong. Almost impossibly so. It's not like her to snap. I want you to know, I want her out of here as much as she probably wants out, but I'm not going to push for it. If you think my visit will cause her stress before she's ready, you need to say so. I have no problem staying away until she's ready."

"I honestly don't know when she's going to be ready. And I'm going to be honest about something else."

"Please."

"I'm concerned that she attacked you because she was harboring some anger toward you. Apparently there was a violent incident?"

He smiled again and leaned back in his chair to one side, as if tucking himself in a corner to get comfortable. He was almost laughing.

The mockery burned me as much as the fact that I had to explain myself. "I'm not talking about anything associated with consensual—"

"This is something she told you?"

"I can't explain further. She came in here with a cracked molar and nerve damage to her wrist."

He pressed his lips together and nodded. Though I sensed a bit of guilt in the expression, it wasn't defensive. It was remorseful and sad.

"Fiona and I have certain rules, and the rules are there for her safety," he said. "Hurting her for breaking them defeats the purpose, don't you think?"

"So she did break some rule?"

"These rules aren't arbitrary."

"I understand."

"I'm sure you do."

From his tone, I could tell he was sure I didn't understand at all, and he was right. I didn't. Not one bit.

"Fiona needs to channel her energies," he said. "What we developed together does just that."

"What's in it for you?"

"Are you psychoanalyzing me, Doctor?"

"It's hard to resist."

He laughed. "All right," he said, sitting straight in his chair. "I'll give you a gift for your honesty. South African farms are far removed from each other, and when I was younger, we had so much privilege, it never occurred to us to protect them. Until, of course, the situation in my country changed. There were too many unemployed young men for the government to deal with, and these young men, they were angry. They were angry at families with money and land. So they gathered in groups and went into the farmhouses and took what they wanted. The farmers were armed usually. My father was, but he was a peaceful man. Of the seven men who came into our house, he shot only one in the leg. He paid for his kindness with his life. My brother was locked in the basement while my mother and sister were badly abused. Our workers... the people were beaten bloody. Two died. I'd grown up with these men. They were my friends."

"Were you there?"

"I was in Queenstown on business, and one of our foremen came in the morning to tell me. He was covered in blood. By the time I got there, it was too late." For a moment, he stared into the middle distance.

I didn't interrupt with any of the hundred questions stewing.

"What happened right after is irrelevant," he said. "But I am serious about protecting what's mine." He smiled, and his smile ended the discussion. He was very shrewd, very self aware.

Plying him further seemed like a waste of time. I was already missing a meeting at Alondra. More small talk would force me to miss an appointment with a patient.

But who was I kidding? Sure, I needed to get out of there, but I'd already assessed whether or not he was a threat to her. What was at the front of my mind, what made me react in ways I didn't understand, was that he loved her. I couldn't pretend to understand how their relationship worked, but when he said her name and asked about her, when he looked at me as if deciding who I was in her life... He cared about her more deeply than I understood.

"Let me talk to Fiona," I said, standing. "Then I'll get back to you."

"Thank you for your consideration."

When he stood, I saw him slow for a second as he shifted. He'd been stabbed in the chest almost two weeks before with a wide, thick blade, yet he'd shown no signs of injury until that moment. Even then, it was

use.

so slight I knew no one who wasn't trained to observe people would have noticed it.

"You'll be restricted to the grounds," I said. "And I'm sorry, but you'll have to be supervised."

"Of course. Wouldn't want her to crack another molar."

He didn't seem the type to joke over something so serious, but the fact that he had sent a chill up my spine.

chapter 17.

FIONA

I skipped lunch to sit at the window. Karen went down to sit in front of a plate of food because she had to, but no such requirements were made of me. I could stare into the grey winter sky and wait.

Deacon was everything to me. What a sad turn of events that someone with a perfectly functioning brain, identified as gifted in third grade, should let her life revolve around a man for her sanity; an unreliable, overcommitted man at that. Worse than a doctor or a cop, there were times he couldn't be around, and I was ill-equipped to deal with them. But that was my fault, wasn't it? A strong woman would have been able to manage during his absences without fucking around, without pissing him off, without breaking every single rule.

But what other man would tolerate my needs? Who else would work with them instead of fighting them? What other person could help me function the way he did?

The goal, once I got out of there, was to either remove Deacon from my life or make sure he didn't leave Los Angeles all the time. Or something between those impossible poles.

I shifted in my chair. The pain in my right wrist ran to my inner elbow. I'd been leaning on it for too long. When Deacon had pinned it against the wall, it had hurt.

But the day he'd showed me how to hold my arms for a knotting, he said that it wouldn't hurt. I'd only realized later that I'd damaged it, so I had to be extra mindful of where the ropes fell before I went into subspace.

He'd knotted me, that time after he returned. The last time. A simple shrimp tie during play, and I'd cringed when he moved my arm.

That was off. If he'd damaged my arm when he pinned it, it wouldn't have hurt until later.

I rubbed my arm. It might never heal. He was very serious about the wrists. Would he have pinned me? Even in anger? And had he held my arm long enough to really injure it?

The soup of questions didn't confuse me, but as I dug into the memory of what happened, it became clear.

***

His breath falls on my cheek, and a pain in my arm runs from my wrist to the sensitive side of my bicep.

"You did not let someone else knot you," he says from deep in his throat. He's naked, stunning. He pins me to the wall, the friction making the open skin on my ass scream.

Regret. Pounds of it. Miles wide. Regret to the depth of my broken spirit.

"I'm sorry." I am. I'm devastated and ashamed.

"Why?"

My wrist hurts. He's pressing it so hard against the wall, as if I'd leave, as if I'd ever turn my back on him. Yet I want to get away, to run, to show him that I can abandon him the way he abandons me.

I wiggle, but he only presses harder and demands, "Why?"

"Get off me!"

"Tell me why!" His eyes are wider, his teeth flashing as if he wants to rip out my throat. "Why?"

"I need it!" The words come out before I think, and they're poison to him.

Before I expect it, he grabs my jaw, and I feel pain where his fingers press. He looks into me, cutting through me with his eyes, and I want to curl up into a blackened char of desiccation.

He lets me go, and I fall to the floor.

***

I almost missed Deacon come out of the building. The valet handed him his keys, and he took them without moving his face from the window. He looked concerned. I didn't know if he could see me since I'd leaned back in the chair, thinking about the last time we'd been naked together.

He stood still, looking up at me. He wouldn't move out of the driveway until I acknowledged him. It was all over his face and posture. I leaned forward and put my finger to the glass. Seeing me, he smiled and put up a finger.

He needed me.

chapter 18.

ELLIOT

I used to be happy at Alondra.

Maybe I was freakish to think of it that way. It was impossible to explain how working with such troubled people made me content, but the small victories looked so large. Then I went to Westonwood, and wound up feeling as though the small victories were the same no matter who the patients were. I felt as if the world was full of too much pain to soothe.

After I left Westonwood then went back, I didn't want to be anywhere, and I wanted to be everywhere. My discontent flourished in a garden of anguish and brokenness.

I'd left my chaplaincy at Alondra and put away the collar. I put off ordination over God's sadistic torture of his only son, and subsequent torture of millions of people, because what was the point of salvation if you still existed at the whims of God and man? What was the point of faith if you were still subject to suffering? I understood all the theologies, but I didn't see why I had to align myself with it. I understood the idea of God as compassionate observer, healer, and strength. Those were all nice ideas. But why choose to stand by them as partner? Why become a mouthpiece?

My mentor, and old horse who never wrote down a sermon in his life, told me I was scared to wear the collar, and though he said it kindly, as if it was totally normal, I'd stormed out of the office.

He was right of course. A step away from becoming a man of God, a commitment I'd always wanted to make, and I ran like a coward. I had no excuse besides fear and an unwillingness to conquer it.

I dried myself after my shower, putting my day together in my mind. Therapy, then a session at Alondra, paperwork, and a quick meeting at Westonwood to discuss scheduling. I couldn't do this for long. I couldn't hold down two jobs. The commute was deadening. Alondra had to go and Westonwood had to go, but I needed them. Everything I was doing, I was doing for the wrong reasons. I was proving to Jana I could do what I wanted by being at Alondra, and I was sating some indefinite hunger by being at Westonwood. I still didn't know what I wanted.

Jana came into the bathroom, her long hair tangled from sleep, her nipples poking through her cloud-and-kitten pajamas. "You done?"

"Just about."

"You going to that place today?"

"That place? Yes." I hung my towel and stood naked in front of her.

"My father is worried about the gangs again, since you're back at Alondra." She turned toward the mirror. "He wants to get us an alarm system."

"No." I moved her hair from her neck.

"He'll pay for it."

"I'm not living in a cage." I kissed the back of her neck.

She shrugged me off. "It's not a cage." She ran her fingers through her hair. "The triggers are so small. You can get one so the alarm just notifies the police. It doesn't even make a sound here."

Her wrist looked so delicate peeking from her pajama sleeves, so vulnerable, with a little gold chain around it. Nothing was more feminine than the wrist. Between her exposed throat and the bracelet, I was fully erect.

From behind her, I wrapped my fingers around her wrist and pulled her arm down. I whispered, "I don't want an alarm system."

I pushed my dick against her and pressed her wrist to her lower back. She tried to pull away, but I held firm. Her resistance sent a wave of pressure between my legs, and something else came to mind. Something that shouldn't have been there while I was trying to seduce Jana.

"I want it," she said.

Was she talking about the stupid alarm system? I didn't care. I had a head full of pink ass cheeks and paddles, of bound wrists and begging.

"You'll get it." I bent her over the vanity.

"Elliot, really…"

I held her wrist with one hand and yanked her pajama pants down with the other. Her ass— unblemished, round, perfectly soft in my hand— creased as I grabbed the flesh.

"Ouch. I have to go to work. What are you doing?"

She wriggled under me, and I held her down. "Something different. Tell me how you feel about it." I slapped her ass. "Later."

"Elliot!"

I slapped her ass again. The sound and the sight of pink finger-shaped marks on soft skin swelled my cock against her.

"I'm at Westonwood. You should be happy." I slapped her again.

She squealed. "What are you—?"

Slap.

"I'm getting ready to fuck you."

She looked around at me, as if checking to see if I was the man she lived with. I couldn't do this much longer or I would come all over her back. I put my dick against her. She was wet. Very wet. And she hadn't told me to stop.

I pushed inside her, and I twisted her arm behind her back, pressing her to the vanity, when I felt her shudder. Her mouth opened a little. Her cheeks flushed when I moved inside her. God, she'd never felt so tight. When I slapped her ass again, she clenched around me.

I leaned over her, letting her wrist go as I curved my body to hers. "You get tight when I spank you. Did you know that?"

I pulled her a little away from the sink and put my fingers on her clit. I'd never handled her so roughly, and I wanted more. I wanted to bite her shoulder. I wanted to pull out, pull her onto the bed, and drive her crazy for an hour. I wanted to tie her up and call in sick. I wanted control over her body as I've never wanted anything before.

But she wouldn't. Not this girl. No time. Got to get to work. Got to argue. Got to talk about fear.

I teased her clit. She stopped pulling away.

"I'm not getting an alarm system, and I'll work wherever I want," I said. "The next time you suggest anything, I'm tying you to the bed with your legs in the air, and I'm going to spank you and tease you with my tongue until you learn who's in control here. Do you understand?"

"No, I don't." The truth was in her moan, not her words.

"Let me be clear then." I buried myself in her, pulled out, and slammed back in.

She clenched and grunted, coming with a gasp and a long vowel, stiffening under me. I lost control of my own imagination which, for some reason, had fixated on Fiona in the afternoon light, moving her finger against my desk blotter. The sexless cut of her shirt made the knobs of her nipples even more prominent, lips over her teeth in a half smile.

I let myself want those nipples. I let myself want to fuck her mouth. I let myself picture her under me, her red hair splayed on the pillow and wrists tied above her.

I came so hard, I thought my body had expanded to the size of the room, pulsing against the walls, the towel rack, the ass pressed against me. I collapsed against Jana, my girlfriend of two years, and kissed the soft skin of her neck.

When she spoke, she did it softly. Not hurt or upset, just matter-of-fact. "Get off me."

***

Jana showered immediately after. She stayed in long enough to make it impossible for me to see her before I left.

So I drove.

When I was ten, I'd woken from a nightmare and tiptoed into my parents' room. We'd just moved to Menlo Park from Fresno, and I was scared of everything. My mother, who seemed more and more withdrawn. My sister, who was growing breasts and curves, changing in ways that made me feel the loss of a friend and the fear of a new creature that I didn't understand. My father, however, was the same. Bigger than life, never arguing or raising his voice, he was a lion whose power was in his gait and mien. I looked just like him in the end, but I knew that power he had wasn't mine to wield.

On the night I dreamed of toilet bowls overflowing with reams of shit, I'd run to Mommy and Daddy's room. I saw them. Mother and Father on top of the sheets, him taking her from behind like an animal. The noises. God, the adult in me had to laugh. I'd been through that memory a hundred times, how he had his hands on her throat. The way he hit her bottom. My mother, groaning.

I'd run back to my room, as if the terror outside it was greater than the terror inside, and curled up, trying to pretend my erection didn't exist. Hadn't I sought God for the same reason I shut my eyes that night? To bathe my mind and soul in light and goodness?

Right in my bathroom, I'd just replayed the whole scene, lick for lick. Why? Because of Fiona Drazen and her coyly baited nuggets of dirty talk. I wanted to be angry at her for it, but I couldn't. I knew better. It wasn't her; it was me.

I wasn't sure I could continue to be Fiona's therapist, and I was positive I couldn't stop. She had abandonment issues, and my leaving the first time had sent her into a tailspin. Leaving again would only reinforce her idea that she was worthless.

Yet my sexual fantasies about her were affecting my life, and seeing her only reminded me that I wanted her. I kept thinking *just once* and *maybe after she gets out,* neither of which would help her.

I kept imagining her body twined with mine, her pink ass, her willing submission, her tiny breasts under my palms. I wanted to taste her. I thought about it whenever I got into my car. Whenever I stepped into the shower. She was like a ghost hanging over me.

"Countertransference isn't about the patient," Lee said.

"I can read a textbook any time."

"You're being hostile. You know as well as I do that you have to look at your own life and decide what needs aren't being addressed that you're imagining she can fill."

"I met her partner. He's an interesting guy. Grew up in South Africa. I think I've been out of the United States twice."

"You talk about him like he's competition. She's not a conquest. She's a patient."

My sessions with Lee had gone from chiding, pleasant, and slightly annoying to highly uncomfortable. I wanted to run away, but like any good therapist, I stood astride my discomfort and observed it.

"I want to just feel something without turning it over constantly," I said.

"That's not your job," she said. "I have to tell you, I'm getting concerned about you. This is dangerous territory. Wanting to explore feelings like this without scrutiny? Come on. What's going on with Jana?"

I didn't want to describe our post-shower fuck. It was too wrapped up in feelings and fantasies Lee would want to spend the next twenty minutes uncoiling. And it didn't matter. What mattered was *why* I was having those feelings and fantasies. What mattered was the situation before Fiona Drazen ever walked into my office.

"I think the worst thing I ever did was cave to what she wanted and work at Westonwood. I'm carrying around a ton of resentment. And the pressure hasn't stopped; she's just moved it to something else. I mean, you'd think we were compatible. I worry. I cope by being organized. She worries. She copes by being organized. But it's deadening. I find I'm the one who's trying to be unsystematic, and I'm not good at chaos."

"Then your problem is with your own life. Please, I'm begging you, don't jeopardize your career by confusing that with redirected feelings for a patient."

chapter 19.

FIONA

"You seem different," I said.

Elliot smirked from behind his desk. He did seem different. He sat a little straighter maybe, or was nervous, or more relaxed. I couldn't put my finger on it.

"I'm the same," he said. "Maybe you've changed."

I shrugged. "Sure, I guess that's why I'm here."

"You saw Deacon come in yesterday, I presume?"

"Yeah."

"Well?" He smiled. "You know what I'm going to ask."

"How I feel about it? Fine. Great. When can I see him?"

"First I want to talk about your injuries. Your tooth and wrist."

"I don't think that memory was real," I blurted. "You said that I could create false memories under hypnosis, and I think I did. You said that the made-up stuff always favors the person remembering, and I think that however I got hurt, I was doing something I wasn't supposed to do. Like, something really bad. So I made the other thing up."

"That just points to you being afraid of him."

I sank a little deeper into my chair. I was afraid of Deacon, in a way. I was terrified he'd leave me and I'd go crazy without him. And how did that jibe with my growing pipedream of being normal? I swallowed hard. I didn't want to even think about it, much less talk about it.

Elliot leaned forward. "Here's my problem. It's my job to make sure you're safe for as long as you're here. It's very difficult for me to let you see him if I believe he's hurt you, or that he will again. If I think he has some sort of unhealthy control over you, and if I think that'll affect your treatment, I can't allow it."

"What do I have to promise?"

"I'll take your firstborn."

A wisecrack was the last thing I'd expected, but it was exactly what I needed. I put my forehead to my knees and groaned. "Take it. I don't want kids anyway."

"It's a deal," he said.

My head shot up with surprise.

"Tomorrow morning."

"Oh my God," I said, "can I kiss you?"

"No." He stood.

I stood as well and looked down at my pale blue psycho suit. "Fuck."

"What?"

"Does he have to see me like this? I mean, it's bad enough I'm here, but I look like a janitor."

He looked at me, toes to crown, as if I was a real woman with curves under my clothes and a choice about what I wore, then took his eyes from me and looked at his hand on the doorknob. I pretended I'd imagined the sex in his gaze.

"All right," he said as he opened the door. "I'll see if we can arrange some normal clothes for you."

chapter 20.

ELLIOT

My belief that Deacon wouldn't hurt Fiona wasn't
based on any kind of data, but on instinct. He might
have an unhealthy control over her, but I didn't think
he was an immediate threat. I feared that if I didn't
allow him to see her, I was preventing it because I
wanted her for myself. After my session with Lee, I
could at least think the words.

I wanted her.

I couldn't do a damn thing about it, but I would
call it what it was. I would look it in the face and say
"no" with conscious intention. I would want her until
she stopped being my patient, then I would forget her
and deal with Jana as if I'd never met the beautiful,
vibrant, decadent heiress.

"Hello?" Jana's voice came over the phone,
crisp and taut.

It was dark as I pulled onto the freeway, making my choice to call her even more stupid. Maybe I felt a little suicidal. "I'm going to be late."

"How late?"

"I have to run an errand."

"Thanks for telling me. Um, can you come in tomorrow to meet Mary? They really need to hire someone."

The school counselor position. I'd never given her a new resume, but Jana must have smoothed it over.

"I'm working at Westonwood in the morning," I said.

"You aren't at Alondra until two. Maybe you could squeeze it in? Think how great it would be to work together. We could have lunch together every day in the break room. It would be like a vacation."

I changed lanes, giving myself a second to think, but I had no way around it. The school was the third option that solved everything. "Sure. Noon should work. Thanks."

"Okay, see you in a bit."

"Okay."

"I love you," she said.

"I love you too." I hung up.

**

There was only one Maundy Street in all of Los Angeles. It was a block long, at the crown of hills above Beechwood Canyon. I twisted up the treacherous slope, back and around, only seeing the headlights of oncoming traffic a second before the car got close enough to hit. To my right, the landscape got longer and longer, the city stretching beneath in a plaid of lights.

Maundy had three houses on it, all behind an iron gate. I stopped the car in front of the gate, my headlights illuminating the houses and trees. All were on the left, facing the view. The house closest was the smallest, and the lights were off. Number three. The house in the center had a few lights on. The back house had huge double doors and hooks in the front facade.

An intercom and keypad were set into the gate, but my lights had alerted the occupants of the middle house to my presence. A slim Asian woman in a mandarin collar walked down the hill. As she got closer, I realized she was barely a woman at all, just at the beginning stages of adulthood.

"Hi," I said. "You must be Debbie."

"Yes, Doctor Chapman?" She shifted the bag to her forearm and pushed numbers on her side of the gate. I heard a *clack,* and she slid the gate open.

"Nice to meet you," I said.

"How is she? Are you allowed to say?" Debbie asked.

"Better. Thanks for the clothes."

Smiling, Debbie handed me the bag. "I packed her something comfortable. If she doesn't like the shoes, she can complain later."

I was tempted to open the bag and see what shoes she was talking about, but I didn't want to walk away just yet. "Do you have a minute?"

She looked me up and down, as if assessing the danger I posed, then slid the gate all the way open. "Pull in. I'll be out in a second."

She went to the small house in the center. I went back to my car to drive through. When I was in, the gate closed automatically. I got out. The door to the little house was still closed, but it wasn't as small as I thought. Only the top was visible; the rest was built into the hill.

I approached the last building. The front windows were covered from the inside. The hooks I'd seen were lower than I expected. Hooks to hold plants were usually above the doorframe, but these were about seven feet off the ground, and more hoops than hooks. Beneath them were smaller U-shaped loops that looked more functional than decorative.

That was number one, Maundy. Of course I should have left it alone. I should have let Fiona's descriptions, which were heavy with her emotions, suffice as a matter of principle. But I couldn't stop myself from walking around the house.

The windows on the side were less carefully covered. Maundy was a private street, so I could understand why they weren't sealed all around. Had the street been subject to any kind of traffic, they would have had to brick up the windows.

A huge room with a floor-to-ceiling window overlooked the mountain, and along the wall I could see, wooden Xs were bolted to the tufted wall. There was a line of chairs that couldn't be called chairs. They were more cushions configured in a way I couldn't understand until I imagined human bodies on them, crouching, kneeling, legs up, spread, arms back or above the head, shackled down with another body. Then their function became clear. The tables for observers only highlighted the fact that the window looked over Los Angeles if anyone cared to watch.

Had that been safe for Fiona with her paparazzi-magnet lifestyle? Why had no pictures of her strapped to U-shaped mattresses and wooden Xs surfaced? Screaming, wet, come-dripping pink-slapped skin, begging for more more more?

"That big window facing the view is one-way," Debbie said from behind me. "You can see out, but no one can see in."

I jumped as if she'd caught me fucking.

"It's the first thing anyone asks," she continued. "You imagine you're seen, but you're safe. It's got to be safe, or it doesn't work."

"Good to know," I said.

"Obviously, the side windows are two-way, but the coverings are sealed on the inside when the house is in use." She smiled, hands folded in front of her. "Come on in." She stepped aside so I could take the stone path to the center house.

The center house was stunning, if understated. Two floors, a modest pool, large windows, and a balcony where I sat on a sofa spanning the length of it. The patio overlooked a terraced yard, the lights of the city, and the black ocean. On one of the terraces, in the dotted lamplight, a slim figure danced, flinging her long, straight hair. No, she wasn't dancing. She was doing some sort of martial art.

Behind me, an indoor light went on, illuminating the figure. I saw the bare chest and loose black pants. The dancer was a man, and he was working with a sword. He moved it with grace and beauty, like a gymnast with an apparatus. I couldn't see him well enough to tell more, but his practice was hypnotic.

Debbie brought out a tray of tea.

"You didn't have to," I said.

"I already had it steeping." She sat across from me on a wicker-and-metal chair and pressed her legs together while she poured.

"This is a fantastic view," I said.

"Yes. I take it for granted, but whenever someone new comes, I'm reminded."

"Do you live here alone?"

"With another student. Martin. The middle house is for functions only, and in the end house, the shibari master lives." She said "master" with a sort of reverence I admired.

"Deacon."

"Yes."

"And Fiona?"

"Yes and no. She's here when he's here. When he's not, she's not."

"May I ask why?"

"You may ask." She sipped her tea, giving away nothing, telling me I could ask, but I'd better be ready to hear something I didn't like.

"Is that Martin?" I asked, referring to the man below.

"No. Junto is mine. Martin was removed just before Christmas. He hasn't been back since."

"Martin was in Los Angeles the days before Fiona went to the stables?"

"Yes, why?"

I shook my head. I didn't know why that rankled, but it did. "I thought he was gone. I don't know why it's relevant. Probably isn't."

But it was, because Fiona had mentioned that time in session.

Even if I was so stoned I'd let them knot me, well, Debbie wouldn't have disobeyed, and Martin was in New York.

Fiona had a memory of being tied while Deacon was away, and had no idea who had done it. But from what I could see, if Martin had been in town, he was the knotter.

"I reported all this to the police," Debbie said. "I knew something was wrong that night. I could tell. Fiona ran out of the house with a bag. I stopped her and asked what was wrong. She was crying. She said she was going to Snowcone. When I saw Master Deacon later, I asked him what that meant. He went to get her." She stopped and looked at Junto, as if clicking pieces of the night in her mind. "Master

Deacon told me I shouldn't feel responsible for what happened. But sometimes I do."

"Anyone would have done what you did."

"You care about her," Debbie said.

I almost choked on my tea. She watched me sidelong, her gaze suddenly pointed with intention. I felt as if I was being taken apart and scanned.

"She's my patient. So yes, I do care." I was sure she saw right through me. "What about you?"

"Fiona is one of the few friends I've made since I came here. She is very loyal, very strong. When I came, I had nothing. Deacon pulled me from hell because he recognized something in me. And Fiona was right there, making sure I had everything I needed. She introduced me to important people. They're a beautiful couple."

"What did he recognize?"

"I'm a female Dominant."

"Ah."

"And good with knots." She smiled into the rim of her cup, still dissecting me.

"I've been told you're very talented."

"I have skill with certain things. The most difficult knottings involve multiple strands. Anyone can tie two, but tying three, from crotch and over the shoulders, it's hard to get them to work in harmony. It's hard to make it strong so that each works equally. But I've been taught by the best." She put her cup down and changed the subject by changing her posture. "Do you run to get clothes for all your clients?"

"Not usually, but I wanted to see this place. Her life here is part of who she is, and I've had trouble imagining it. It's been a block for me. I can't understand the day-to-day."

"You're curious?"

"Not necessarily."

"I can get you an invitation to an event."

"No." I couldn't have been more definite about crossing that line. It would damage Fiona's trust in me completely.

"Really?" She obviously didn't believe me.

"Really. I'm just here to learn about Fiona."

She sighed. "Is it breaking a trust for me to tell you what everyone already knows? It's in the news every night. The public feeds off her like birds on suet. And she doesn't have the upbringing to stand up against it. No grounding."

"She's had a very traditional upbringing," I said. "Her folks are religious. She has seven siblings to lean on."

"She has a wire mother."

I sat back, considering my tea. The study she referred to involved removing newborn monkeys from their mothers and putting them in the arms of a chicken-wire figure that dispensed milk. "Are you referring to the Harry Harlow experiments?"

"I'm sure I don't remember the name of the doctor. But I saw a film of monkeys clutching a wire mother and biting each other. Almost all of them, in one way or another, was a sexual deviant. It was hard to watch."

"That study showed that a newborn without attachment to an adult has a higher chance of being impulsive and violent," I said. The experiments had been inhumane and horrifying. Human babies rarely faced that level of distance from all adult love. But the point had been made that a wire mother permanently damaged children. "And what's your theory on what this has to do with Fiona?" I hid the stress in my voice. I'd always seen Fiona as someone with solvable problems. Debbie apparently thought differently.

She folded her hands in her lap, calmly considering me. "The babies had no warm mother, but they were given every single other comfort they needed. Even more than they needed. What happens when the child of a wire mother is given every indulgence, and then has to deal with the slightest pain? Does the pain break them? Or are they already broken from the pleasure?"

I leaned toward the railing and looked over the city. The man with the sword had stopped his dance. He sat cross-legged, facing the same direction I was, with his hands out in supplication.

"When she looks out into the world, she sees only herself," Debbie continued. "She has a large family with wire parents. Those children are a brood of rich orphans. The fact that she can eke out as much humanity as she does is beautiful to me."

I felt the friction of my middle finger on my upper lip before I even realized I was rubbing it. I shifted my hand down. That habit triggered my mind's gears, no matter how much I didn't like it. Her parents still hadn't visited to tell her about her brother. They were leaving it to the children to sort out amongst themselves. Had it always been that way? Had something else broken her? Did there need to be more?

Everyone had a bucket that represented their capacity for pain. Some buckets were bigger than others, and everyone maintained the overflow differently. Did it matter that Fiona's bucket had been filled slowly, drip by drip, over years, if she hadn't been given the tools to manage the runoff?

"People are terribly complex in their simplicity." My general statement wouldn't betray any confidences, but it was possibly that simple. Or not. I had enough to chew on.

"I'm glad you came by." Debbie placed her cup carefully back on the tray. "It was nice to meet the man who is helping Fiona. She's a good person with a good heart."

I stood. "Nice to meet you as well."

We shook hands, and I left. I dropped the bag of clothes on the passenger seat, but I was halfway down the hill when I couldn't take it anymore. I had to know what she'd packed, what she expected Fiona to wear.

The zipper on the bag screeched when I opened it. The shoes were in a separate drawstring bag. They were white sneakers with Velcro, plain and simple. Was it wrong that I found them so sexual in their pure plainness? The lack of sensuality, the creases at the backs where they'd been smashed. The way the tongues were off kilter. The back heel of the left shoe was more worn than the right. She favored her left foot. It was the sexiest thing I'd ever seen.

I was having intimate feelings for a patient by way of a pair of running shoes.

I jammed them back in the bag without looking at the clothes and zipped it up, declaring to myself that I'd never look at them again. But it wasn't the sneakers that were the problem. It was me. I was the problem.

chapter 21.

FIONA

Jonathan seemed obsessed with physical activity. He wasn't at the ping-pong table when I went looking for him after dinner, but he was on the basketball court under the lights. His motions were much the same as they'd been with the paddle: dribble twice, then a *whoosh* into the net. He caught the ball and started over. The grounds were populated with all kinds of psychos huddling in little groups under the lights and in the dark corners of night. None went near Jonathan. He was a red menace all his own. Mister Joker. Mister Tons-of-Buds.

I leaned on the pole that held the hoop. "Making friends, I see."

"I have you, Fee." *Swoosh.* "I don't need friends." He smiled.

I hadn't expected any kind of cheer from him. "Who removed the stick from your ass?"

"Guy can't catch a break. What am I supposed to do? Have another heart attack?" He took his shot. "And how are you doing? Try to attack your therapist lately?"

"Not lately, fucktard."

He passed me the ball, hard. It took the wind out of me, but I caught it.

"Twenty-four hours of self-control," he said. "A personal best for you."

Jonathan was back. The guy who couldn't stand me, who ribbed, chided, and pushed my buttons until I either stormed off or slapped him.

"And you?" I said, passing it back as hard as I could.

He caught it without a problem and dribbled.

"You aren't some great example of self-control. If I want that, I'm looking at Theresa."

"She's gonna bust one day." *Swoosh.* "Leave a bunch of lace and pearls all over the place." He made an exploding gesture with his hands. "Boom."

I caught the ball on its way down. "She said she's sorry she got mad at you, by the way." I tossed it to him. "She called you names, apparently."

"I don't blame her. But yeah, she lost it. From now on, I'll be a model of having my shit together. Anything I can control, I will. Done. And sorry, Fee, but I'm staying away from you. You're a bad influence. Staying away from Dad too. He's worse. He makes me want to break his face." He took his shot and missed. Retrieving the ball, he said, "Control. Everything in my line of sight."

"You think it's so easy?"

"Yeah, I do. It's a choice. I can see crazy coming now. You. Then Rachel. Then me. I know the signs now. I got it." *Bang.* The ball went off the rim. "I'm watching Theresa next. Margie's on her way. We'll all be here at some point until we learn."

I caught his ball mid-bounce. "You're delusional."

"You know who my girlfriend was obsessed with before she died?"

"Jesus?" I took a shot and, *bang*, missed. I was never much of an athlete.

"You." He snapped the ball out of the air. "Talk about delusional. She thought you were the shit. Thought you had the life."

"Why?" That knowledge poked me in a weird place. I was many things, but admirable wasn't even on the list. Yet, a swell of unexplained intimacy throbbed around the admiration when I was sure I'd never met Rachel at all.

He bounced his ball but didn't take the shot. "She was a normal, regular girl. Bad family, but otherwise, she was real. The way we live was like a fairytale to her." He laughed and bounced the ball until it flew over his head. He caught it and dribbled again. "When she saw how you lived, the way you spend money, she admired it. I should have caught it then. I think what bothered me the most when I heard about her and Dad was that I hadn't seen it. How did that shit slip under my radar? I don't like being blind. I felt like I got it in the back of the head with a baseball bat. Then, the party, and I wake up, and she's gone." He took a shot. *Swoosh.* "She was real, and then… not."

"Because she wanted to be us."

"Crazy fucking world," he said, passing me the ball.

I stood in front of the net and tossed the ball up. By some miracle of chance and physics, it went *swoosh.*

"Nice shot." The male voice came from my left.

I turned to find Warren Chilton palming the ball I'd let fly.

"Drazen," he said, flipping Jonathan the ball.

"Hey," Jonathan said back.

I was sure he was trying to place Warren's face. Warren was about seven or eight years older, but there was a good chance they'd pulled smoke from the same bong, somewhere. Jonathan took his shot, missing because he seemed cautious in a way he hadn't before. He passed it back to Warren.

"Where have you been?" I asked, returning to the pole as Warren jumped for the hoop and missed. *Bang.*

"I had a dispensation to go to my sister's wedding. Got the ankle bracelet off with a blowtorch and bolted." He lifted his pant leg, revealing a red, raw burn wound.

"Wow, dude." Jonathan dribbled, staring at Warren's ankle. "Where'd you go?"

"Stole my dad's car and went up to Santa Barbara."

"Cool." He flicked the ball to Warren, who missed the net again. I couldn't believe Jonathan would be impressed with the high drama, but he was sixteen.

"Wasn't even a blip on TMZ. You guys are still eating up all the bandwidth."

Jonathan laughed as his rebounded Warren's miss. Warren fouled Jonathan and bounced into me, shoving a little baggie of blue oval pills into my hand. I tucked them into my waistband as he winked at me.

"What's on the news about us?" Jonathan said as he passed to Warren. "Anything that'll get me laid when I get out?"

I glanced around to see if anyone had seen me tuck away the baggie.

"Fiona," Frances called to me.

I turned. She was standing next to Elliot. They waved me over.

Shit.

chapter 22.

ELLIOT

I could see she was on her best behavior, hands in her lap, sentences short and spoken softly. Her effort to not come back at us appeared monumental, and I was proud of her for keeping it together in front of Frances and sympathetic to how hard it was to seem awake when saying "yes" and "no" when she wanted to say so much more.

"Do you understand the rules for tomorrow's visit?" Frances asked. She spoke to her peers with bite and wit, but she spoke to patients as if they were children.

"Yes," Fiona said, looking each of us in the eyes from across the conference room table, the same table we'd betrayed her at two weeks earlier. "One hour. Just talking. No going outside the garden area. You'll have a guy on us the whole time."

"Miss Drazen," Frances said, softening her voice slightly, "I hope you don't feel persecuted. We're trying to make sure this is a safe visit. This man is the reason you're here, for better or worse. There is violence in your past together, so we have to be careful for your good and the good of the other residents."

"I get it."

"It's only Doctor Chapman's word that makes this possible."

She glanced at me. "Thank you."

"My pleasure," I lied.

***

Jana was cleaning up the dishes when I got home.

"Hi," I said.

"Hey." She was mad.

I was far later than I should have been, but I'd needed to update Frances on Deacon, and then she insisted on a conversation with Fiona. The explanation was on the tip of my tongue, but I bit it back. I counted the dishes. "Who was here?"

"I had Mary come to talk to you about the job. I figured I'd kill two birds with one stone. But you didn't show up, so…" She shrugged and picked up her wine glass.

"We're meeting tomorrow. You can't dump an interview on me twelve hours early."

"If you were serious in general, you would have been here, home with me. But now you look unreliable, and I'm embarrassed."

"That's unfair," I said.

"What were you doing?"

"Working."

"Is there someone else?"

"What?"

"Are. You. Fucking. Someone. Else?" She said every word slowly. She'd had a glass too many, making her words wet and thick with emotion.

I crossed the room in two steps and removed the glass from her hand before it reached her lips. I pushed her up against the refrigerator and held her by her sternum. With my other hand, I reached up her skirt.

"Why?" I asked with my lips against her cheek. "Have I come home with the smell of pussy on my face?" I pushed past the crotch of her panties and jammed two fingers inside her.

She gasped. It couldn't have felt good, and I didn't care.

"Lipstick on my collar? Have I called you another name?" I dug my hand against her, pressing her clit.

"What are you doing?" she squeaked.

"I'm taking you." I added a third finger. She was wet now. I slid them out and against her clit, then back inside. "I'm tired of this shit. There's too much talking and not enough screaming."

"God, what—"

"Say my name."

"Elliot," she moaned when I stroked her clit.

"Again."

"Elliot."

"When I say to get on your knees, get on your knees." I stroked her clit, gathering moisture around it gently. "I'm going to drag you to the bedroom by your hair and throw you on the bed. Get on your back and spread your legs." I put three fingers in her again, roughly, digging down to the knuckle. I had no idea what I was doing but telling a story of the next half an hour. "Then I'm going to bend your legs at the knees and kiss inside your thighs. My tongue will go from one knee to the other, stopping at your pussy for only a second. Then thigh to thigh. Then I'll land on your clit. I'll kiss it and lick it until you beg me to fuck you."

I had her. She was wild, with hooded eyes, and her hair was in front of her face. When she looked at me, I was sure that when I said *get on your knees,* she would. I was rock hard, waiting for it.

Instead she said, "Is this how you talk to her?"

I stepped back, pulling my wet fingers out of her. I'd intended to put them in my mouth in front of her, but now they felt sticky and dirty. "Forget it. Just forget it."

"I can't shake this feeling there's someone else." She adjusted her clothes.

"I'll be in the guest room." I wasn't supposed to stalk off into the other room and close the door. I was supposed to keep communication open, but I couldn't, because I didn't even know what I wanted from her. I didn't know what I felt. What could I expect when I came at her like that after an evening looking at a BDSM playroom?

I should have opened my heart to her. I could have told her that a new part of myself was opening up, even if I didn't understand it. But I didn't want her to know. I wanted to stew in my desires without volleying someone else's needs.

This was mine.

chapter 23.

FIONA

By the time I went for my nine o'clock session, I was jumping out of my skin. Deacon was coming at eleven. Two more hours. I'd already put on my jeans and blouse, laughing at the unsexy, dowdy shoes.

"Who picked these?" I asked Elliot. "You?"

"Debbie."

I laughed again. "She and I used to joke that these were the least sexual type of footwear in the world. She obviously thinks I need to tone it down a bit."

"Is there a way to be who you are without thinking sex is all you're meant for?"

I didn't even know if I could answer him, because his fingertips on the blotter were making me crazy. How lightly they touched it, as if enjoying the warmth of the leather. I tried not to stare, but I kept seeing his hand out of the corner of my eye and hearing the light rustle of his touch. I wanted to finger myself in lieu of trying to seduce him, because he was unseduceable. I was lower than a rat in a sewer to a guy like him.

"I'm not ashamed of what I am, so I never thought of needing 'more,' if you know what I mean," I said. "I would show up at Maundy and strip down to my underwear. Deacon would leave my stuff by the door. When I put my ankles in the leg spreaders, it was like my job. I did it, and when I got turned on, it was just me doing what I was meant to do. I walked to Deacon's room, and he'd be waiting. Except it's not like I could walk in the spreader, so I'd tip or do something wrong. That was also my job. To fuck up so he could tie me down with my legs open. To beg when he asked. To be a whore for him."

Elliot's finger stopped stroking the leather, and he swallowed. If he stood, I would have seen a rock-hard erection. That was also my job.

"You take a lot of pleasure in talking about sex," he said.

"I do."

"I need less of that."

"Why?"

"Because you're trying to arouse me, and I want to keep being your therapist."

"I'm not trying," I said.

"Please try *not* to then."

"I'm a fucker. It's what I do."

"You're not. You are not defined by sex."

"I'll define myself any way I want." My voice was shot through with defensiveness, and I hated it. He made me feel as if I'd wasted my precious time doing and learning things that were worthless. "I'll decide what about me is worthwhile. I'll decide what I talk about and what I do."

"You're not deciding. Your addiction is deciding."

He was so confident he was right, and I felt a swell of violence I had to quell. I was T-minus ninety minutes to seeing Deacon. I would not be baited by a sexually frustrated motherfucker who wanted to rip away who I was. My lip quivered with the effort, and my eyes filled with tears. I resisted the urge to tell him how grateful he'd be for my skills if I got my lips around his cock for five minutes.

"Do not tell me who I am," I whispered.

"I don't know who you are. But I know who you're not." He slapped a box of tissues in front of me. "You're not a mindless, heartless 'fucker.' Maybe you should listen to the people around you talk about you. They don't think you're a bag of sex either."

I ripped a tissue out of the box as if it had personally offended me, which it did. Fucking tissue. I blew my nose in it. "I decide, okay? I decide what goes and what doesn't. How other people see that, I can't help it. People get hurt, you know, it happens, but I don't lie. Everyone's on board."

"Everyone? You just said people get hurt."

"Sometimes."

He moved his notebook out of the way and leaned on his desk as if I'd said something he wanted to latch on to. "Tell me the first time someone got hurt."

"The last time was Deacon—"

"Not the last time. The first time."

"The first time was my fault."

"Okay. Let's hear it."

I didn't want to tell that story. I didn't want to say what I'd done, how careless I'd been. But Elliot had come back for me, and I said I'd play ball. So I just had to spit it out, didn't I?

"Evan. I won't use his last name, because you know his father. I mean, not know know, but know."

"That's fine."

I cleared my throat. Could I just pretend he wasn't there while I told this story? Like maybe I was lying in bed, staring at the door to the bathroom as the sun came up. "So summer after high school graduation, I'm dating this guy Evan, who's going to Brown in August. We don't have a permanent thing, because he's leaving and I'm just going to UCLA. And so he's fine and all, but his best friend Gary is pretty hot, and he's staying in town. So I suggest to Evan that it would be fun for the three of us to get together more or less at the same time."

Why was I hemming and hawing? Why was I using soft words? That was bullshit. I held my chin up and rephrased the last part. "I told Evan I wanted a threesome with his buddy Gary. It hurt his feelings. He said no, because he liked me for a girlfriend. I hadn't told him I wasn't girlfriend material."

"And he broke up with you? How did that feel?"

Fucking feelings already? Jesus. "It felt nothing because he didn't break up with me. Not until later. Not until... He went to Brown anyway, so it didn't matter."

"So he stayed with you for the summer?"

"Why do you want so many details?"

He shrugged. "If you'd stop skipping things, I'd stop asking questions."

"What makes you think I'm skipping things?"

"It's my job."

Fine.

Fuck him.

"After Evan said no, Gary invited me to his place. Which was fine, because fuck it. If Evan was going to get his knickers in a bunch, fine. But Evan was there. And I think, *This is not a threesome. This is not them being cool with it.* Because there's no drinks and there's no drugs, and the music is off and all the lights are on. So I'm like, 'Hi, guys, what's up?' Evan makes a dumb comment like, 'my dick' or some dumb jock thing like that, and Gary..." I stop, because I feel my face crunching up.

Elliot lets me sniff and get it together.

"Gary pushes me. He puts my face on his kitchen table. He does it hard. So I'm like, 'Get off me.' But Evan, he comes around and yanks down my jeans. And then… I couldn't move, because Gary was holding me down. God, I can't tell you."

"You don't have to."

But I needed to. I needed to fucking finish it because I'd told my therapist I'd play ball. Just because I had fantasies of a normal life with that therapist didn't mean anything had changed for him. I was the one who had to just get through it and do what I said I'd do.

"I'd never had anal before. I didn't know you have to lube a lot and do prep and you have to be really turned on. Evan didn't either, because he just opened up my crack and spit, which is never enough… God, it hurt. It hurt my ass, and it hurt my insides. And he wouldn't stop. I kept saying, 'Stop, stop. You're hurting me.' Gary wouldn't let go, and Evan kept doing it. After he came, they switched places." I stopped. I wasn't crying because I'd shut off all my emotions. If I let them out, I wouldn't have been able to tell the story to the object of my silly, normal fantasies.

"I'm sorry that happened."

His face was ice cold, as if he didn't care. As if it was one of a hundred stories he'd heard about a girl getting ass-fucked twice with a mouthful of spit for lube. Just another patient with a stupid story. That was all I was.

"It was my fault," I said. "See, I did face consequences once."

"For what? For wanting to explore your sexuality? For wanting to move on from a relationship that wasn't going anywhere? No, Fiona. No."

"Well, fuck it. I said never again. From then on, I was crystal clear. I'm not anyone's girlfriend. I fuck around. Period."

"So you can never have non-consensual sex if you consent to everything?"

"If you want to put it that way," I said, crossing my arms. I had to hold back tears when he said it though.

"That's brought you to quite an impasse."

"It was working really well."

"Until it wasn't."

"Yeah." I sniffed. If he was trying to empty my head of snot and fluid, he was three quarters of the way to me opening the valves.

"I spoke to Debbie when I got your clothes," he said softly. "She talked about you as if you were a real person. One with honorable qualities."

"Debbie sees the good in everyone."

"She said you helped her acclimate when she got to Maundy."

I rubbed my nose. "She's very young, but she didn't need me. She's plenty mature. Martin would tell you what I am, and how good I am at it. But you wouldn't believe his opinion because you don't already agree with it. Right?"

He paused too long. I took that as a victory. I'd stumped him with his own relativism. I didn't stick my middle finger in his face and piss on his desk, but I felt that good... until he spoke.

"Martin wasn't in New York before Christmas. You said he was away when you were knotted by someone else, or something like that?"

I felt myself blink. Felt a skip in my brain. He was right of course. Martin hadn't been in New York. I knew that. So why did I feel as if a mental drain was clogged?

I felt a shot of pain in my tooth. I put my hands over my mouth, because neurons that hadn't fired since the stables connected again, and I was afraid that memory would fly out of my head.

"Martin. He knotted me while Deacon was away. Oh my God, that's worse than fucking him. That's why he was so mad." The words spilled out of me with the memory.

Hanging, the sway of the ropes in a deep fog, and the ceilings, a pale blue instead of Deacon's wood beams. I wanted it so bad, but his hands were wrong. They pulled at odd angles, unsupportive when I needed it, and my stomach roiled with alcohol and drugs. The colors blurred, and the rough hemp ran on my raw skin as everything under me fell away before the lightning bolt crack of the floor.

"Martin was sloppy, and he dropped me. I fell on my face, and my wrist was tied all wrong. I didn't feel it because I was fucked up on something." I pressed my fingertips to my cheek, where the damaged molar was. "Deacon really didn't hit me. I thought he might not have, but I didn't know what to believe anymore. But it was that dumb shit."

"The dumb shit who knows what you should be valued for? *That* dumb shit?"

I didn't say anything for a minute, maybe two. It took me that long to shake the surprise.

As if he could tell when I was ready to hear it, Elliot said, "I told you the memories you called up under hypnosis would be colored. What was important were the feelings you unearthed. You weren't afraid of Deacon when you remembered him hitting you, and that's important. But you colored the event to absolve yourself of guilt for breaking the rules with Martin."

"What about the stables?" I said. "What did I change there?"

"You're going to have to ask Deacon."

I nodded and folded up my tissue.

"We have two minutes," Elliot said. "I'm taking those to give you a task. When you talk to yourself about yourself, I want you to try something new. I want you to use different words."

"Like?"

"Like loyal. Strong. Trustworthy. Spirited. Brave. Selfless. Use those words, Fiona. Stop lying to yourself about who you are."

chapter 24.

ELLIOT

I didn't know when my emotions flipped during the
session. If I hazarded a guess, it was when I gave Fiona
that box of tissues. I defined her not just to her but to
myself, and speaking those words, I saw past all of her
bullshit and my own arousal. In asking her to define
herself, I'd done the same in my own mind, and I knew
how deep my trouble cut.

Then when she told me she'd been raped by her
boyfriend and his friend, my detachment went to hell.
I'd heard a hundred more violent stories, yet I wanted
to find those two men and eviscerate them for hurting
her. I hoped for Fiona's sake that I'd kept my shit
together.

I heard her brother one rec room over, banging
on a ping-pong ball. But in this room, it was quiet.
Patients read and chattered softly. This room had a
window overlooking the drive. It was my turn to watch

and ask myself how I felt when the black Range Rover rolled past the gate.

I felt insignificant. I felt lost in a whirlwind. When Deacon Bruce handed the valet the keys and I stood in that fucking window like a stalker, I felt like a pebble in a shoe, waiting to get shaken out and discarded. When he looked up for Fiona and saw only me, I felt as if my heart was being squeezed. He saw me and waved. He knew what I was doing. He knew he had what I wanted, but he wasn't worried. I was the also-ran, the second place, the beta in a pack of wolves. I waved back as if accepting my position.

How did I feel?

I felt as though I was going to be late. I felt the weight of my responsibilities to other people shedding from me. I walked to my office which overlooked the garden, and on the way, I pulled my phone out of my pocket. I barely paused as I called Jana.

"Hey, are you—"

"No. I'm going to be late." I spoke quietly and tersely.

"How late?"

I'd used the wrong word. I'd shuffled and shimmied when I should have just stated the facts. "I'm not going."

"Should we reschedule?"

"Cancel it. And I'm not discussing it further. I'm sorry. I don't know what I'm going to do, but I'm not working at Carlton Prep."

"Elliot, we agreed."

use.

"You agreed. I have to go." I hung up and pocketed my phone.

There would be painful repercussions to just about every decision I'd made in the past thirty minutes, but they were the best decisions I'd made in the past two years.

chapter 25.

FIONA

In the end, I wore the psycho suit with the sneakers.
On the one hand, I was sick of their damn
indoor/outdoor Velcro slippers. On the other, I didn't
want to be different. I didn't want to hide what I was
from Deacon. I was troubled, and he knew it. I knew it.
Jeans and a blouse wouldn't change that. So I wore the
sneakers remembering the laces under the Velcro, like
a bit of adulthood hidden under the child-safe
fastening. I never bothered to unlace and retighten
them. I'd rather jam the back of the shoe down and
pivot my foot as if I was doing the twist.

And I wore the panties, because I was sick of
the gross, disposable mental-ward underwear that rode
up my ass.

I sat in the lobby, running my fingers over the
damask. Peeked out the glass doors. Then stood and
looked at the three-foot-high fresh flower arrangement.

Then sat in front of the wood-burning modernist fireplace. Then peeked out the glass doors.

He wasn't late, ever. Not that he fussed about it. He owned a watch as black as his car and as big as a dinner plate, but he always seemed to know what time it was without looking.

I, on the other hand, looked at the wall clocks as if they ran backward when my back was turned.

He was coming.

I knew that he hadn't hit me. That I'd let Martin knot me, which was forbidden because it was dangerous and just another instance of infidelity. I knew nothing about the stables except that I'd been startled when someone came in, and Deacon knew everything. Only he knew the level of my betrayal, and only he could forgive me.

Behind me, a closet door slammed. Mark, the pierced orderly, came out.

I'd slammed a door that night. I jumped when I heard a car door slam outside.

Deacon. He was here.

I'd slammed the door on the way out when I'd gone to the stables. I left in a rage, warring with my shame and self-loathing.

It was him, the man walking toward me in a black wool jacket and flat-front trousers. Him, with the blazing blue eyes that had seen so much and the hands that could grasp, inflict, caress all at the same time.

He'd left me for letting Martin knot me. No, he hadn't hit me or broken my tooth, that I'd done to myself, but he'd kicked me out.

use.

***

"Empty your heart, my kitten. Empty your mind. Open your eyes. Who do you see?"

Deacon yanks my hair back until I'm looking at him. I feel at home and excited. He's back. He was gone, and he's back.

"You," I croak.

"Are you empty?" He pulls my arm back and stops.

"Yes," I say.

But the fluidity of the moment is gone when Deacon rubs a sore spot on my wrist with his thumb. He's behind me, on his knees, his throbbing cock at my crack. I don't want him to rub my wrist. I want him to fuck me.

"What's this?" he asks.

I thought the bruises were gone, but Deacon has an eagle eye. No detail has ever slipped by him, and no lie has ever gone undetected.

"A bruise." I intercept the next question because he already knows the answer. "From rope."

He leans back, and I know it's over. He's not fucking me. He'll forgive me, but he won't fuck me.

"Who?" he asks it as if it's relevant.

It's not. Someone else knotted me. We reserved that for each other. I stand, because I can't admit this while in a submissive posture. I have to hold up my head. Have to.

"Martin. He wanted to work on that last asymmetrical pose."

"Was Debbie there?"

"No."

"And?" He's standing now, hard as a rock. Terrifying.

"And what?"

He won't ask me if I fucked him, because that's secondary. He's just going to stand still with a look of shock, and then he's going to step forward in a way that makes me step back, once, twice, until the wall prevents me from going farther. His breath falls on my cheek, and a pain in my arm runs from my wrist to the sensitive side of my bicep.

"You did not," he says from deep in his throat. He's naked, stunning. He pins me to the wall, the friction making the open skin on my ass scream.

Regret. Pounds of it. Miles wide. Regret to the depth of my broken spirit.

"I'm sorry." Am I? Or am I just saying that?

"Why?"

My wrist hurts. He's pressing it so hard against the wall, as if I'd leave, as if I'd ever turn my back on him. Yet I want to get away, to run, to show him I can abandon him the way he abandons me.

I wiggle, but he only presses harder and demands, "Why?"

"Get off me!"

"Tell me why!" His eyes are wider, his teeth flashing as if he wants to rip out my throat. "Why?"

"I need it!"

use.

*He breathes once, heavily, as if filling his lungs
to say something he doesn't want to say. He reaches
for me, and I think he might say it's all right. He
brushes his fingertip across my bottom lip, and I'm
about to burst with gratitude. His face is soft and
loving, and he's mine as much as I am his.*

*"I'm sorry," he whispers. "You have to go. I
can't trust you."*

*I'm still in shock when the door slams behind
him.*

***

I watched him sign himself in with my hand
over my mouth. He was there, breathing the same air
as me. He'd come. Maybe he hadn't come on a white
horse to catch me as I jumped from a tower. Maybe we
weren't going to ride off into the sunset, but he'd come
for me.

He'd come for me.

I kept repeating those words, awash in gratitude
to him, to Westonwood, to Elliot, to the people who
built his car and pumped his gas.

He came through the glass door. It whooshed
and breathed when it closed, and he stopped when he
saw me. I was a wreck, and I knew it. But I wasn't
worried about how I looked. Nothing could be further
from my mind. It was never about that between us,
because he saw *me*.

I didn't have a word or a gesture to express
how I felt. I kept my hand over my mouth so I didn't

spit when I cried. He took four steps, big ones, across the length of the hallway and wrapped his arms around me, lifting me off the floor. He smelled of hickory and leather, adventure and brokenness. He smelled of pleasure and pain given without regret, and when he held me tight, I felt both.

"Fiona," he said as if expressing longing and hope.

"I'm sorry," I said through my tears. "I'm so sorry."

chapter 26.

ELLIOT

I closed my office door and went to the window. I waited like a spider waiting for the web to vibrate, arms stretched, owning my vulnerability to her, the fact that I wanted her and someone else had her.

It wasn't long before they came out and sat on a bench. When he put his hand over hers, I felt how Fiona felt. Worthless, consumable, a cold faraway planet circling a brilliant sun. That was my pain. Mine. No excuses. I would steep it in boiling water until it bled out of the bag and colored me the dark, opaque crimson of shame.

chapter 27.

FIONA

I pulled Deacon outside like a kid showing off her dollhouse.

"And we have one guy here I went to school with. He knows every flower and all its medicinal properties. I mean, he's nuts, but right? You can't help it." I walked backward to the patio.

"You're not nuts, kitten. Haven't I told you that?"

"God, it's so nice to see you."

"Nice?"

It was session time, so the rec room was empty. I was a fucklot happy about that, because I didn't want anyone to see us. What we had wasn't public. It wasn't meant to be shared by sight or smell. The next hour was ours. Fuck all of them. I wanted every curious eye the fuck off me.

He put his arm around me, and we walked out into the yard. I pulled him to a bench halfway between the building and the treeline. He didn't take his eyes from me. We were like a long-separated couple who couldn't imagine being in each other's presence again. He sat next to me and twisted to face me, bending one arm over the back of the bench and putting his other hand over mine.

"You look beautiful," he said, and he never, ever lied.

"You too. Like no one ever stabbed you."

"It wasn't that bad. A flesh wound. Two Band-Aids and mercurochrome. Kiss it and make it better. Nothing."

"You were in the hospital."

"A luxury hotel."

"The knife missed your heart by how much?"

He shrugged. "It missed."

"I don't need you to forgive me," I blurted. "Even if you did, I'd never forgive myself. For everything. For letting Martin work with me, for trying to kill you. Everything."

His hands were so tender on mine, I felt as if they'd break the bones.

"You don't remember anything?" he asked.

"I've just started to remember that night at Maundy, when you threw me out." I choked a little on the last part. "I'm not saying I blame you."

"How are you?" It wasn't a polite question or small talk. He wanted a real answer.

"I don't know. I keep looking for an answer from other people, like they're going to tell me how I am. I feel myself wanting you to tell me if I'm okay. I didn't realize that was what I expected from you, and you know, you can't tell me. No one can, but... this is crazy."

"I'm ready."

"I don't know how to talk to myself, so I'll listen."

He laughed, not with humor but recognition. "You are more brutal on yourself than anyone else." He put his fingers on my lips.

I tasted him, and the desire to open my mouth and take him down to the knuckles was overwhelming.

"I think we hurt each other," he said. "I asked you for monogamy for the wrong reasons, and that's what started the whole thing."

"If it's what you want, it's not wrong. I can try again."

He shook his head. "I thought you wanted it. But I don't need you to be exclusive. I don't get jealous of other men as long as I know them and know you're protected. I thought it would make you happy. I thought you'd be safer if you were completely mine. But it doesn't. It makes you trapped. It makes you do stupid things. I'll never ask that of you again."

"I can."

"Well, then do it. Just do it, if that's what you want. I haven't touched another woman since you, and I won't. None of them are interesting to me. But that's my choice. It has to be your choice too. I can't impose it on you, and I can't punish you for who you are."

He couldn't punish me for who I was. A whore. A fucker. A sex bag with no goals, no worries, nothing inside her. But he didn't mean that. I knew he meant I was some sort of life-giving spirit-goddess above the care of mundane things like fidelity, but he was cutting me.

"You mean that?" I said. "You mean you could just let me swell and fuck when you're not around, and it'd be okay with you?"

"I'm probably the only man in the world who doesn't get jealous at that thought, but you have to be you. I take you that way or nothing. You know what you are to me. You're my reason to feel good. Even after everything, when I think of you, I'm happy. That's all I want, to feel that freedom. I'm not interested in the baggage that comes with enforced exclusivity. Kids, marriage, the myth of the happy home. None of it is for us."

He'd said it before, and I'd embraced it then.

"I want to ask you something," I said, casting my eyes down.

"Yes?" He raised an eyebrow. He knew what I was going to ask; I'd bet the entirety of my trust fund on that.

"Can you tell me what happened? How I stabbed you? I can't get my head around it."

He looked away. In profile, he looked thoughtful, statuesque, with a bump on his nose where it had been broken and his chin at a right angle to his neck. "There's no point, me narrating a story, is there? You need to remember."

"I can't."

He leaned in. "You can." His voice got low, turning breaths into words.

When he spoke like that, I could understand him no matter how loud the music was. I shook my head with a sting in my sinuses, tears borne of shame.

"I can help you."

"By telling me. Please."

"No, I can help you remember. Do you want that?"

I nodded. Fuck, he was so close, breathing on me, his stubble so near I had to twitch to feel it. "Yes."

"We need to be alone," he said.

"What do you have in mind?"

He raised an eyebrow. He had no intention of telling me. God, I loved him. The power he carried in his bones, as if everything in his reach would be all right. No wonder I fell apart when he went away.

"Okay," I said. I didn't mention that being alone was against the rules or that breaking them could keep me incarcerated longer than either of us wanted. "Wait here."

He leaned back, and I got up. I glanced at Mark on the way to the bathroom, jerking my head toward the inside. Like a good little monkey, he followed me, catching me outside the door to the ladies'.

"What?" he asked. "You doing all right?"

"I need to be left alone by the fence."

"With the guy?"

"With the guy."

He crossed his arms. "I could get fired for that."

"I'll make it worth the risk."

"You ain't that good, baby."

I should have put a little more effort into our bathroom encounter. That would have made for an easier negotiation. "Five grand when I get out."

"Ten."

"Seven. No more bullshit. You're not the only orderly in here."

He considered that for a second, probably spending the money in his mind.

"And I gotta have the guy at the monitors turn the camera. He could get fired too."

"Five for him."

We were taking too long. I already knew I was being watched, and talking to Mark outside the bathroom would be noticed anyway.

"You gave pretty good head," he said.

"Jesus, you're a pig."

He seemed to like that. I should have called him a gentleman.

"My cock needs sucking, dollface. I'm on night shift, and it gets a little boring watching you whack jobs beat off."

"Fine. Just take care of it." I pushed my way into the bathroom before he could demand my ass as well.

Karen was coming out of a stall. "That Deacon? The guy on the bench I saw you with?" Her breath smelled of puke. Her voice and gait were weak and drowsy.

"Yeah."

"Wow. He's like… I don't know the word. Powerful, maybe? Jesus. And those eyes."

"Yeah. He's great on the inside too." I didn't have to pee, so I just straightened my hair in the mirror. I needed a minute for Mark to do his thing.

"Good for you," she said, going for the door. "You could use a break."

"Thanks." She was about to open the door when I said, "Can you keep away from the holes by the creek?"

"Sure. Everyone's in session, more or less. You should be fine."

I held the door open for her, because she was having trouble with the weight of it. Mark was across the room, moving a tray of medication. He saw me and winked. A little nod of his chin told me what I needed to know.

I went outside. Deacon was waiting for me, a beautiful streak smeared on a miserable landscape. I held my hand out for him.

"All taken care of," I said.

"You have real skill."

I pulled him into the garden. "You have no idea."

"Don't I?"

He did actually, but I didn't want to tell him I'd just spent twelve grand and promised a distasteful blowjob in exchange for thirty minutes of privacy with him. I would have spent more. I would have tacked on more money and let that pathetic fucker come in my ass a hundred times just to be with Deacon.

"Here we are," I said when we got to the chain link. A new hole had been opened. "Not glamorous, but it's what I got."

He pulled the hole wide. "Go on."

I slipped through, and he followed, getting his wide shoulders through the narrow opening without mussing a stitch of his clothing or mellowing his intensity. I felt as if we'd crossed some sort of threshold together. He stood straight above me, and I knew there would be no more talking. No more promises. No more sweet words. Not until we'd slipped back to the other side of the gate.

My heart pounded. "Master, may I speak?"

"Go ahead."

"We need to stay on the other side of this tree if we're going to be out of the camera's range." I kept my eyes on his shoes. I was trying not to smile with joy and excitement. "If that's what you want."

"Take your shoes off," was all he said.

I slipped them off and handed them over.

"Good girl," he said. "Now go to the other side of the tree. Pull your pants down to mid thigh, spread those pretty legs, and wait for me."

Breathless with anticipation, I walked my socks to the other side of the tree. With my back to the trunk, I hooked my fingers under my elastic waistbands and pulled my pants and pretty cotton underwear halfway between my crotch and my knee. The forest air hit my ass and my wet cunt like a slap. I put my hands at my sides and stretched my legs as far apart as the clothing would allow.

Deacon was there. I tingled all over with that thought.

But he didn't come around the tree right away. He spoke from the other side. "Pull your shirt up so I can see your tits. Hold it there."

He knew my tits weren't big enough to hold up the shirt, so I was left with my hands on the hem, showing myself to no one but the Deacon-to-come, the specter of a promise soon to be fulfilled. My nipples stood erect, and my pussy seemed made of pulsing blood.

Deacon came around the tree soon after. A shoelace was draped over his arm. He had a sneaker in his hands. The Velcro was pulled back to reveal the lace underneath. He yanked it out hole by hole. *Whup. Snap. Whup. Snap.* The laces were quite long. I could have hanged myself with them easily.

"Debbie told me you were babbling about taking care of something that night. She described a leather bag you were carrying that she'd never seen before, but I knew was your horse grooming kit."

"I don't—"

He slapped me across the tits. The sting was delicious.

"Let me finish." He grabbed my jaw tightly. "I'll ask a question when I want one answered."

"Yes, Sir," I whispered.

"She said you told her you were going to be a grown-up for once. So I went to get you. I was angry." *Whup. Snap. Whup. Snap.* "I didn't want to be manipulated, and Fiona, make no mistake, you can be manipulative." *Whup. Snap.* The last bit of shoelace was free. He dropped the shoe and ran the laces through his fingers. "But Debbie was worried which, from her, I take seriously."

He looped the laces, knotting them in a way I couldn't detect, and stepped toward me until I felt his jacket on my skin.

"Put your hands on the branch above you. Grab it."

I did, letting my shirt drop. The branch was just above my reach, making me stand on my tiptoes to grasp the rough winter bark. He twisted the laces around my wrists then around the branch, securing me.

"And I found you there," he said, letting the ends of the shoelace drop around my shoulder. "Alone, or so I thought."

I knew better than to speak though I wanted his brutal touch on me again. He wrapped the last of the lace under my tits, squeezing them every time I moved. I felt him behind me, doing the last knot. He yanked on the lace as if he was running out of length, then made it and pushed me. I swung. God, it was blissful. I closed my eyes and went outside myself to a place where I was no one, nothing.

"Look at me."

I did. He was backlit against the speckled canopy of leaves, and his gaze on me was like a caress in hard metal and soft flesh.

He leaned over whispered, saying the words he always said before he fucked me, sending me to a place where I surrender all anxiety to him.

"Empty your heart, my kitten. Empty your mind. Open your eyes. Who do you see?" He took my nipple in his fingers and twisted it.

"You," I gasped.

"Are you empty?"

"I am."

"Release your body to me. I have you. Even in the stables, I had you." He placed my right leg over his hip and said, "Remember."

***

I smell hay and shaved bone. I'm cramped between the horse and the back wall. There's no thrush on Snowcone's frog, and that kind of pisses me off. He's been taken care of like a favorite child, even with me gone. He kicked me two years ago, and I'd walked out, blaming the horse for what the rider should have known.

Here I am again, showing up like I belong here, and he looks at me as if he knows good god damn well I abandoned him for doing what horses do. I hate myself. Disappointment. Deserter. I've been abandoned for being who I am, and I'd done the same to this poor baby.

It's night, which is a stupid time to show up hoping my key still works, but where else was I going to go? Who else would bear me? I had to see if Snowy would take me back. I had to see if even an animal would have me. And I want to do something for him, to repay him for the unrestrained nuzzle. I want to groom and love him. A brush would be fine, but any hand can brush. I want to go an extra mile.

But his hooves are near perfect. He's old, and richly indulged, and unloved.

I need to stop crying. I can't see the frog and the knife isn't pointy, but the edge is sharp, and I don't want to hurt the horse.

I needed to stop crying. Deacon was whispering to me, 'remember, remember, remember.' *His cock's at my opening, and I was sure I would come when he entered me.*

"Fiona? Fiona Drazen?"

Her voice surprises both me and Snowcone. I leap up with my knife, and the horse shifts and clops.

"Who are you?" I ask.

She's in her late teens, and she has long blond hair and muddy eyes. Jeans, zip-front cardigan; she's average in dress, but she has an intensity that makes me wary.

"My name is Rachel Demarest. I want to talk to you."

"About what?"

She steps forward. "I'm a friend of your family. Maybe Jonathan talked about me?"

"No."

"Well, we're dating so…" She twists the ends of her hair. "Theresa? Did she mention—?"

"What's your name again?"

"Rachel. Jeeze, I feel so stupid. I mean, look at the time. You've never even heard of me. You must think I'm some sort of stalker."

"You looking for a picture or something?" Maybe if I snap a picture with her, she'll go away and I can go on swimming in my own shit.

"No. I'm just… How can I say? Um, I just… I was meeting Theresa at your sister's. Sheila, I mean. She's having this Christmas party, and we're helping set up. It's right by the water." She waves vaguely west, to the shore edge of Rancho Palos Verdes. "So Theresa mentioned that you had a horse in these stables, which are, like, just over the hill, and I've been thinking of riding again so… God, this sounds just awful."

"How is Theresa?"

She shrugs. "You know, perfect."

Her eyes don't roll, but her tone matches a snarky eye roll, and I feel a little more comfortable with her. Theresa makes me want to roll my eyes too.

"This is a beautiful horse." She approaches Snowcone with her hand out and strokes his neck. "He's a hotblood?"

Deacon's cock slid in and out of me while I was tied to a tree, his voice in my ear. He told me over and over that it was all right, that he had me. I felt his arms around my waist, his hips holding me up, the swelling heat between my legs.

"Arabian."

He was so good. So perfect. He took everything away.

"Gorgeous."

"My brother's girlfriend, huh? Sorry. I haven't talked to the little fucker in a long time."

"I'll tell the fucker you said hello."

I laughed a little, letting go of a slice of my sadness and loneliness. Maybe I needed to spend more time with friends. Maybe that was the way to forget about Deacon.

"I think you're amazing," she whispers so softly I don't know if she's talking to me or the horse. "You're so composed. So confident. Even when they come after you the way they do."

"I don't feel so confident." I sit and get back to Snowcone's hoof.

He huffs and fidgets more than he did before. He doesn't like two people handling him. Was he always that way? I don't even know.

"Hey, Rachel, could you—"

"I thought I could be someone like you."

"Just take a step back while I finish up, okay? He's skittish."

She does, and Snowcone calms a little. I'm in control. I have this. As empty as I feel, I take this as a good sign.

"I wanted to go to an Ivy," she says. "I have the grades. Did you know they give a ton of financial aid?"

"Really?" I let his leg down.

"But I can't get any. My parents make too much, but not enough to actually pay the tuition. Isn't that funny? And here's my boyfriend, who could pay with his pocket change."

I don't have an answer for her. I already feel like shit. I put the knife on top of the kit while I put away the stool. I slip past her, my back grazing Snowcone's side in the tight stall. In that second, from the way she looks at me, I know I could have her right there. Why not? What does anything matter anymore? All this pain could go away for a second, cocooned in a silky knot of sex.

"Master." He fucked me full, pushing himself against my clit. I was a white swirl of pleasure. "I'm going to come."

"Have you remembered?"

"No, but—"

"Then you may not."

I kiss her, because she's there and I'm an addict. Addicts don't give a shit. Addicts are only concerned with pausing their own pain. I put my tongue in her mouth and grab her hair, yanking it. She kisses me back, groaning and pushing her luscious tits on me. I put my hand up her shirt, under her bra, and run a thumb over her nipple. She gasps. Snowcone shuffles.

"Are we going to fuck or what?" I say.

"I've never—"

"Gotten your clit sucked by a woman? Oh, honey, you've never been licked and fingered until a woman's done it." I bend my knee between her legs, pressing against her cunt.

She grinds against me. "Jonathan... Don't you care about him?"

So close to her face, I see a flash of something in her eyes. Something less than innocent. Something more experienced than she's letting on. I pretend I didn't see that. I can't think about her motives, because I have a need and she's going to satisfy it.

"He'll get over it," I say.

"Remember, kitten. I have you." He was so tender.

I was crying and close. I cried for the careless bitch I was and the fact that I didn't feel changed at all. Who deserved me? Not even my family deserved such a reckless whore.

"I'm sorry," I said, more to everyone I'd ever fucked over than to Deacon.

"You're forgiven."

I yank her pants down and get my finger on her pussy. She's soaking wet, a slippery mass of flesh I know how to navigate. When I touch her clit, she squeaks. I'm in control; I have this bitch. I can make her cluck like a god damn chicken or come like a queen.

I take her hand and put it flat against my belly then push down. "Come on, touch it. It feels just like yours."

She bites her lip and timidly touches my clit.

"That's right," I say.

She runs circles around the hood, making me groan. I hook my fingers in her hole and press the heel of my hand to her clit, sliding it back and forth. She looks at me with her mouth open, eyes hooded.

"Don't come," Deacon said.

"Don't come," I say.

"I don't think I can stop."

"I can't stop it."

"Stay with me, Fiona."

"Stay with me, Rachel."

"I—"

"I—"

"I have you."

"I have you."

"Fiona?" It's Deacon's voice, and then it all happens very fast.

Rachel screams in surprise. Enormous pressure on my back as Snowcone bucks. Deacon's voice. Rachel letting out a war cry as she pushes me away. The horse slams me back toward her. Deacon grabs the bridle. Rachel has the knife, and I hear her scream, "I hate you! I hate all of you!" She thrusts for my face, and I can't move. The horse and wall are in my way. I move. She misses, but I'm cornered. Deacon shouts something I can't hear over Snowcone's bucking and neighing.

The horse moves.

I fall.

She's on top of me.

"He'll kill you. Your brother. Your cunt's all over my hands."

The horse's feet clop around me. They could crush my head. But Rachel is so mad, and she doesn't know.

"You're all going to pay." She's laughing. Crying.

Where's Deacon?

Snowy's losing it.

It's loud.

The paddock shakes when Snowcone rears.

The hoof knife falls toward my face, handle first.

I roll, missing getting my head crushed by an inch.

Rachel is sucked away, backward, clawing for my face. She grabs the knife.

I get my feet under me. Snowcone bucks his rear to the right, into Rachel's knife hand. It drops. I grab it, and I'm confused. Because Rachel is fighting him, and I'm still heavy between my legs. She's calling him a lowlife pervert. That's Deacon she's talking to. He's trying to wrestle her away without hurting her, but we're in this tiny space with a bucking horse. My sexual arousal changes to unmitigated fire when she hits him in the face.

He hurt me. He left me broken and adrift, but he's mine. She can't do that. She can't hit him, because when she does that, sh'se threatening me, my life, my love, my world.

And I have a knife. It's for scraping not stabbing, but the handle is hard in my hand, and she has to get the fuck away from him. She's a wildcat. He's trying to grab her wrists.

"Fiona!" he calls.

I don't know if it's to help him or to get back, but I'm mid swing. I realize why he called my name, but it's too late. Snowcone bucks again, making everything nuts. Rachel is pushed away, and the knife finds its way into Deacon's chest. I yank it out in a reflex. There's no blood. Not yet. He just looks like a stricken man with a ripped shirt.

He's not mine. He's not my world. He just cut me loose to drift into an endless void.

I'm a rush of hormones and endorphins, a slave to my anger and pain. "Fuck you!" I punch his chest. But there's a knife in my hand.

He deflects. The wound is shallow, but it's the one made with intention. I scream.

Though Snowcone seems to calm despite everything, and Deacon at first seems bemused and stunned, Rachel is still pure adrenaline. She pushes me down to get out of the claustrophobic paddock.

Then the blood appears. Deacon's mouth and eyes are open, and they're filled with me. The knife falls. A door slams. Everything goes black.

I felt as though I was going to die. Not die. Cease.

As if my existence was about to be snuffed into a tiny dot as big as the universe and black as the sun. Though I usually dove into the obliteration, I didn't this time. I feared this orgasm as I'd feared no other, until I heard his voice.

"Come, darling. I have you."

chapter 28.

FIONA

He'd untied me and put my shoes back on, kneeling before me as I sat on a tree trunk. It seemed as though hours had passed, but it had only been twenty minutes, plus five for him to take me down and another five for me to tell him my memory.

"I'm sorry, again. I'm sorry," I said.

"You didn't mean it. It was an accident."

"The second one. I meant that one."

"Barely a scratch."

"Deacon—"

He put his fingers on my lips. I needed him to make me suffer, and not within the boundaries of funishment. I needed to writhe from his anger. I needed to feel as though I was dying. That was only fair.

"When I negotiate with the men holding my people, I have to see past their anger," he said. "I have to see their suffering. If I can't see the human inside them who saw their fathers killed or maimed, or if I can't speak to their slow starvation, I can't get to them. I stay on the outside. In order for me to find them, I need to be inside." He put his hand on his heart. "When you took that second stab, I was inside you."

"But those guys, when you negotiate with them, and you find them—"

"They aren't my reason for living." He stood and held his hand out to me. "Once my guys are safe, those men are tools for a message."

I took his hand, and he pulled me up. "So you're not going to have me dragged into the square?"

"Never. Martin, on the other hand..." He didn't finish, just put his arm around me, and we walked to the fence. "Your father. She was trying to blackmail him?"

"That's what Theresa and Margie said."

"I think she needed one of you to speak against your father. She needed you to break apart to do that."

"We'd never," I said.

"Not her, not this time. But you're only human. All eight of you. One day, you're going to fall apart. But not because of me. So I didn't tell anyone about that girl until I had the whole story."

"I think Jonathan would break if he knew."

"I won't tell."

"I know how you feel about the cops anyway. But she's dead now. It won't help anything."

We walked to the fence, and he pulled it open a little for me. I crawled through as a different person, a cleansed one. I was a woman who, if not sinless, had had her gravest sins washed clean.

The garden was quiet. No one had found us. Mark had kept up his end of the deal. Deacon and I walked back to the garden, then to the front lobby. His time was up.

"Deacon, I have something to say."

"Say it."

"I love you," I said.

"I know."

"I don't know if this is what I want. What we have. I don't know. I don't want to lose you, but I can't string you along if I don't know."

He touched my chin with his thumb. "What we have is exactly what you need. Nothing else will work for you. We fix each other's brokenness."

"I don't want to be broken."

He shook his head. "You don't get to choose that. You can choose to let me protect you, and I will Fiona. If you stay with me, I'll stand between you and anything that comes at you. I'll be your guardian and avenging angel."

When he left and I watched him roll away in his black car from the upstairs window, wondereing if I could make it without him. He didn't fix me. He didn't make me whole. He took my broken pieces and gave the cracks between them a purpose. Who was I without that? I shuddered with fear at the thought. I'd be adrift without him, a dinghy in an ocean, but until I faced that lonely expanse, I'd never find land.

chapter 29.

FIONA

The lights went out.

My arms ached from being tied, and the abrasions from the shoelaces throbbed a little. I didn't want to touch myself. My clit had rolled over and gone to sleep finally.

I'd left the bathroom door open a crack. I thought I should close it or the whoosh of the pipes would keep me up. I'd forgotten to take the Halcion. I thought I should get up and take it. I was meeting with Elliot in the morning to talk about whether or not I was ready to be released, and I wanted to be rested. I closed my eyes and thought about the stables, about Jonathan's girlfriend, about kissing and fingering a woman I'd never met knowing that she belonged to him.

That was the old me.

The new me wouldn't do stuff like that anymore.

Someone somewhere flushed a toilet. The pipes whooshed. I considered getting up and closing the bathroom door, but I was asleep before I could.

chapter 30.

ELLIOT

She looked rested. Her eyes were lit with awareness, and her face was alert and reactive. That was the effect Deacon had on her. Much as I wanted to hate him for touching her the way he did or get angry that he had what I wanted, the change in her demeanor could not be ignored.

"I saw you go into the trees," I said. "You were supposed to stay in sight."

She swallowed hard. "Why didn't you ring an alarm or something?"

"It would achieve nothing."

"But isn't that what it's always been?" she said. "People keeping me from the consequences of my actions?"

"Do you want to know the consequences of your actions yesterday?"

"I'd have to stay."

"No. You'd get kicked out."

She laughed to herself and shifted in her seat.

I continued, "It was clear to me, after I met Deacon, that he wouldn't hurt you. I didn't think he'd put himself in a position again where you could hurt him."

Which was partly dishonest. I knew no one was going to get hurt. But I was jealous. Seething. If I'd sent someone after them, it would have been nothing but a reaction to my jealousy. I couldn't let that happen. I was still her therapist.

"Thank you," she said.

"You didn't hurt him, and he didn't hurt you. So keeping you here to keep you away from Deacon isn't enough reason. You're sane and stable enough to face questioning. I don't think we can hold you anymore." I should have been relieved or at least happy, but I was confused.

"When am I going?"

"I have to do some paperwork, but probably in a day."

I gauged her reaction, and it was surprise, not fear. That was good.

"Are you okay?" I asked.

"I think so."

"You look a little shell-shocked."

"I'm scared to go out there. I'm scared of the cameras, and my family, and honestly, I'm scared of myself. I don't know what I'll do, but I have to decide whether to go back to Maundy or not. Right now, I think no. I have to get control of my life, and Deacon was a crutch. When he was gone, then this place became a crutch. I get, right now, why people want to stay in here."

"You should probably continue some sort of therapy," I said.

"Yeah. But I don't live in Compton."

"I can't be your therapist anymore."

"Why not?" She sat straighter, and her voice went up an octave. She was hurt.

I hadn't intended to hurt her. "Because I don't have a private practice."

Because I can't look at you.

Because all I want to do is touch you.

Because I want to hunt and kill everyone who ever hurt you.

Because healing you is personal to me.

Because I'm going to fall in love with you.

"I don't want to talk to anyone else," she said.

"I'll recommend someone you'd like." I stood, buttoning my jacket. "Give yourself some time after you leave before you decide how to proceed with therapy. But not too much."

"Sure," she said, standing.

We went to the door together, and I put my hand on the knob. We did that every time, but this was the last time, and I was slow to open the door. She came close to me.

"Fiona." I said her name as if I was entering another place, another state where words were warmer, and the things I felt didn't have to be locked away.

"Yeah?"

I had to press my lips between my teeth before I said something stupid. I released them when something sane was ready to come out. "I liked working with you."

"You know how I feel," she said.

In her voice… did I hear that same warm place? If I did, was it even valid? "I guess I do, I just…" *Shut up.*

Her hand flicked to the ends of her red hair. As it fell back down, a reflex came straight from my lizard brain.

I caught it.

What the fuck are you doing?

Her fingers rested on mine, and with my thumb…

Don't.

…I brushed the tops of them.

You're breaking a sacred trust.

I looked from the hands to her face. Her eyes flicked back and forth, her lips parted. She was motionless as I leaned closer, like a ship keening on the sea. If I kissed her now…

Your career is over.

She'd open her mouth, and our tongues would touch. I'd taste her. I'd feel her warmth. I wanted to. I wanted her more than I wanted my career. My nose ran astride hers, and I tasted her breath. She was there for it. She wanted me to.

She's probably going back to Deacon.

I closed my mouth and tilted my head to put my lips, and the kiss, out of reach. "I'm sorry." I dropped her hand.

"It's okay."

"No, it's not."

"The other day, when you told me all the words to use to describe myself, you forgot one."

"Really? What?"

"Irresistible."

chapter 31.

FIONA

I ran as fast as I could in those stupid shoes. I was getting out, and even as scared as I was, my joy at my freedom wasn't easily contained.

And there was Elliot. It had been a moment. His thumb on my fingers. His mouth so close to mine at twitch would have brought our lips together.

He wouldn't have me. He wouldn't come near me again, not if his life depended on it. I knew that. But I also knew that a normal man with normal desires who wanted a normal life could, in the short run at least, find someone like me attractive. And in that, a crack opened, and a stream of possibilities poured in.

I barely stopped in front of Karen's room. Discovering she wasn't there, I checked the upstairs rec room. Jonathan was playing ping pong with Warren as if it was a full-contact, high-stakes sport.

"Jon! I'm out tomorrow!"

"Thank god," he said with a *thup crack thup.* "I'm sick of looking at you."

I was about to go down to the cafeteria when I saw the ambulance outside. "What happened? There are paramedics in the driveway?"

Warren didn't lose a beat. "Karen had a heart attack."

Jonathan caught the ball midair. "What? How?"

Warren shrugged, but I knew god damn well what had happened. She'd taken Warren Pharma's uppers to kill her appetite, and her heart gave out. I stared Warren down, and he smirked and shrugged. Jonathan joined me at the window.

"Shit," he mumbled.

I ran downstairs. A crowd stood outside the cafeteria doors, but having clubbed my whole life, they were a permeable barrier, as long as I didn't care who I pissed off.

Mark stopped me. "Hold on. If you're not an EMT, you're on this side of the line."

Past him, six paramedics lifted Karen onto a gurney.

I pushed Mark out of the way and ran to her. "Karen!"

I didn't know if she'd heard me. Tubes were sticking out of her face and arm, and her head was held still by a white contraption. Hands grabbed me. I shook them off until I got to her, and she saw me. Her eyes were half-closed but alert.

"We're friends outside this place. You got it?"

use.

She blinked. She'd heard me. Mark came behind me and wrestled my arms behind my back.

"Okay, okay!" I shouted. "We're good. I'm going."

I stood with my hands up, perfectly still, and Mark stepped back to let me pass.

chapter 32.

ELLIOT

Home. The house I'd bought in a flurry of financial
optimism during an economic downturn. The last bit of
luck I'd ever had.

    The lights were off, but Jana was home. Her car
was in the drive, and I saw the dim flickering of the
fireplace through the front curtains. I'd almost kissed
Fiona Drazen in my office. So much went through my
head, the churning excuses, the feeling of autonomy,
the crushing guilt.

    I dropped my bag at the door and walked into
the living room. Jana stood in front of the fireplace, her
short silk nightgown falling over her breasts like light
pink syrup over a vanilla sundae. Her hands were at
her sides, fingertips tight against each other. Her big
toes lay right over left.

    "Hi," she said.

    "Hi."

"How was your day?"

"Fine. Yours?"

"I'm sorry," she blurted. "For accusing you. But you've been distant, and that was where my mind went."

I stepped close to her, raising my hand over her breast without touching it. If I lowered my hand, I'd feel the nub of her erect nipple under the silk. I'd draw my hand down the fabric until I got to the hem, then I'd reach under and find out what was happening beneath that nightgown.

"I'm sorry too," I said. "I've been distant. You're right."

I didn't lower my hand. If I admitted I had another woman on my mind, the fact that I'd never actually laid a hand on her would be utterly irrelevant. I'd cheated emotionally. If I told Jana that, how deeply would it hurt her, standing there in her pink silk nightgown before a roaring fire?

If I touched that tit, I would fuck her and fuck her hard. I would think of Fiona, and that wasn't right. She'd put on that nightgown for a difficult evening. I couldn't take her with a clean conscience, and I couldn't refuse without leaving her.

I put my hand in my pocket.

She swallowed. "There's someone else."

"No, but..."

"But what?"

"But there may as well be."

Was that cruel? Was there an easy way to do this? Was there ever a good time to tell someone that

your heart had been looking for someplace to land for
a long time, and the fact that it had landed with
someone inaccessible didn't mend the unhappiness?

"What does that mean?" Her lower lip
quivered.

I wanted to take it back, fuck her senseless, and
break up with her later during a convenient little fight
that I'd engineer. But that was the coward's way out,
wasn't it? "I'm sorry."

"You want me to leave?"

"You're a beautiful woman. You're smart and
caring, and… It's not you, it's—"

The slap on my cheek rang my bell. Of all her
fine qualities, I hadn't counted a left hook among
them.

"You are a fucking prick," she said, finger
pointed. "You're a drifter. You haven't been able to
hold down a job since you walked away from your
discernment committee. You don't talk about it. You
don't talk about anything. You only start all this weird
fucking dirty talk. You spank my ass in the bathroom
and expect me to what, enjoy that? And now you have
the nerve to tell me how 'beautiful' I am? And that's
what? Prelude to a break up?"

I noticed that her nipples were no longer
making peaks through the fabric of the nightgown. We
were doing it, right here, right now, breaking up. It was
the right thing, the only thing, and it felt like hell. "I'm
sorry."

"Well, guess what? Maybe I'm not interested in
a guy who'll bring gang bangers to the house. Maybe

I'm not about to let my kids hear you tell me what you're going to do to my pussy by the refrigerator. You've changed, Elliot. I don't know if this is a phase or what, but you've changed."

"And you haven't." I tried to stop myself but couldn't. "You're still a sheltered, scared child."

"You're just pissed off you couldn't fix me. This is not my failure. It's yours."

Everything we needed to say to each other had just been said, but it would go on all night. The beginning parts had gone down easier with a dose of uncontrolled rage.

She stormed into the bedroom, slamming the door. I looked at the ceiling, my hands still in my pockets. She was right about everything, and I was too. None of the obstacles between us were insurmountable. We could work on all of it, stay together, and be happy-ish. But I wasn't willing to climb that mountain. It seemed a long, hard slog for a peak overlooking a view I didn't care to see.

I poked at the fire, moving a log so it would go out sooner rather than later. I didn't feel good about what I was about to do, but it was honest. I stood, replaced the poker, and went into the bedroom to do what I should have done months ago.

chapter 33.

FIONA

I walked back from breakfast drowsy with contentment
after a night of non-Halcion-aided sleep. I was leaving.
A few hours more, and I was free. Free to deal with my
family's shit. My father and his proclivities. My
mother and her constant terrors. My brother's dead
girlfriend. The media.

Deacon.

I was done at Maundy. It had been a chapter of
my life, and it was time to move along and control
myself, my desires, my dreams. My plan was to focus
on riding. I'd maybe train another horse, maybe do
some coaching. I couldn't do that with Deacon
allowing me a life driven by my cunt. When that thing
was at the wheel, every other life's desire went dark.

"Hey," Mark called. He was in his street
clothes, torn black jeans and a black sleeveless
Metallica tee. "You owe me. I got ten minutes."

"You know I can't get money from here."

"I ain't talking about the money."

I rolled my eyes. "Fine. Let's get this over with."

As I kneeled on the bathroom floor and took his cock down my throat while he called me names, I was kind of relieved. Once I got out of Westonwood, I wouldn't make deals like that anymore. Blowjobs weren't currency. I could say no like a normal person and find some other way to pay for what I needed.

Mark wouldn't appreciate the fact that he would be the last stranger who grabbed my hair to hold my head still so he could come on my face. That was all right. He didn't need to know. I needed to know. I had control over my shit.

I wiped his jizz off my eyelid and looked in the mirror at the queen of her domain, master of her universe.

chapter 34.

FIONA

The grounds never seemed so huge as when I was looking for my brother and couldn't find him.

"Warren," I said, approaching a small group of guys, "have you seen Jonathan?"

He looked me up and down, as if assessing more than a lost sibling. "I think he went past the gate for a smoke. Come on, I need to catch up with him too."

I followed him past the treeline.

"So," he said, "I hear you're getting out today?"

"Yeah, I just have to run upstairs and change. I wanted to catch him before second sessions."

"He's around somewhere." He peeled the chain link back for me.

"Hey," I said from the other side, "can you kind of look out for him? Make sure he doesn't lose his temper over stupid shit?"

He slid through. "Sure. He's all right, that kid."

"Yeah, he is." I walked on, scanning for the kid Warren spoke about as if he wasn't close by. "I don't see him." I skirted the edge of the creek. "Maybe he's back in his room?"

"Jonny?" Warren barked, getting ahead of me. "How's the Halcion panning out?" he called back to me.

"Great." I followed him. "Thanks for it."

"Good." He put his arm around me. "You know, you owe me for that shit."

"How much do you need?"

"I have money." He looked at my lips and down my shirt, flicking his tongue over his top lip.

Shit. "Warren, I'm not interested in that kind of trade. Can you think of something else?"

"Sure." He wove his fingers in my hair.

I dropped my arm from his waist and leaned away.

He balled his hand into a fist, grabbing my hair, and pulled me to my knees. "I can think of something else, but it's not what I *want*, okay?"

"Ow! Warren! Stop!"

He threw me onto the ground, and my cheek slapped onto a layer of wet leaves and rock. I tried to scramble up, but he used my forward motion to get my pants down, sliding them to my calves. I screamed, but it came out as a grunt since the wind was still knocked out of me. He threw his weight on top of me and clamped his hand over my mouth.

"Scream." He was breathless himself, holding my mouth with one hand and wiggling his dick out with the other. "Maybe your brother will come. He'll walk away when he sees his whore sister getting it up the ass. Then how's that release gonna work out? You caught here doing what you do?"

I shook my head. I felt the skin of his cock against my butt cheek. "No," I said into his hand.

"I don't hear that. Not from you. You had it in your ass so much in Ojai I can't believe you ever sat again. I'm moving my hand. You scream, and I'll tell them you wanted it. Ain't nothing to me if I have to stay."

My fingertips gripped the soft earth. My ass was already sweaty from being pressed against him.

"I'm moving my hand," he said.

I groaned, not agreeing to anything. He slipped it away.

"Please don't," I said.

"There's some shit Daddy can't pay for." He put his dick between my ass cheeks. I tried to get away, but he yanked my hair back. "Stay still and take it, you little whore."

With that, he jammed himself forward, missing my ass. Undaunted, he adjusted and pushed himself inside. My face contorted. Tears fell. My breath went out of me.

"Oh, you're so fucking tight for a slut."

"Warren, it hurts. Please. Lube me or something. God, fuck."

He pulled out and pummeled me again. "I like it dry."

He hitched my hips up. I was crying as he bore into me.

"I hate you," I growled through my tears. "I'm going to get you for this, you fuck." My face was inches from the ground, so close my breath bounced back into my face.

A caterpillar crawled from under a leaf, his body curling around the edge, changing its shape with as his teeth ate it slowly.

"How much Halcion you got in your blood?" He pounded relentlessly, shredding my ass. "That's mine. I paid for this fuck, little slut. Yeah, take it all the way. You love it in the ass like this. All whores want a dick in their ass. Say it."

"No!" Fuck him. He wasn't getting consent. Not for anything. Not for one stroke.

He put his hands around my throat. "Am I not fucking you hard enough?"

He tightened his grip, and the edges of my vision darkened as he beat my asshole with his cock. I only saw, in a pinpoint of light, the little caterpillar eat his way across a leaf. I waited in the center of my pain for that caterpillar to grow his wings and fly away.

chapter 35.

ELLIOT

Right about lunchtime, I thought about Fiona. I thought about where she was in her day, when she was being released, how she was getting home, where home was, and who was taking her. I thought about her over my sandwich, and pushed it away not because I felt full but too dissatisfied to eat.

Our final good-bye gnawed at me. After I'd told Lee about my eternal night with Jana, as we negotiated the emotional parts of our breakup, I mentioned the almost kiss with Fiona.

"You're kidding," she said, her face white.

"Almost, but we didn't."

"*We* didn't? No, no, you do not put it on the patient when you—"

"She's a grown woman."

"—clearly crossed a line—"

"Nothing happened."

"—taking advantage of her—"

"Come on, Lee. She's gone. It's over. I'll never see her again."

She slammed her hands on the desk. "Do not absolve yourself of responsibility. I am stunned, stunned at what's gone on."

"You're losing your professional countenance."

"I'm livid for her. The fact that you can sit there and make lame, embarrassing excuses for totally inappropriate behavior sickens me. I know I'm your therapist. I'm supposed to sit here and ask you how you feel about what did or didn't happen, but I don't care how you feel." Her face was beet red, fists clenched, her unborn baby getting cortisol by the quart. "I'm enraged for the entire psychiatric community."

"Then fuck the psychiatric community entirely."

I'd walked out in a tight ball of anger, unable to see a past opening my car door, getting in it, and turning left out of the lot. Right. Right. Left. Straight. Around the corner to Alondra, where I sat with my sandwich, wondering what Fiona was doing in her last hour before release.

I couldn't see her. Lee had been right, if unprofessional in her delivery. The therapist and patient had a relationship based on the therapist's power. By using that power inappropriately, I'd broken a wall that had been erected for a reason. A good reason.

I crunched up my paper wrapping and told myself I wouldn't see Fiona again. I exited the lunch room to get to the paperwork I needed to finish before I went home to my empty house.

Minutes later, with the paperwork undone on my desk, I got in my car. Naturally I was going home. I was too distracted to fill in little boxes and put together sentences coherent enough for insurance companies and government agencies. As a matter of fact, I thought, as I turned south on the 110 instead of north, I didn't think I could ever do that work again.

As I went west off the exit, deep into Rancho Palos Verdes with its exclusive horse-and-pony enclaves, lawyers' mansions, actors' estates, winding roads around nature preserves, and of course, facilities for the mental health of the very monied, I thought I could do better than that paperwork. So much better.

As long as I kept my hands off the patients.

chapter 36.

FIONA

I couldn't cry.

If I cried, I wouldn't stop. They'd see me and ask me what was wrong, and then everything was a crapshoot.

If I cried and managed to stop, I'd have puffy eyes, and they'd ask me what was wrong. Then I wouldn't know what came next.

So I didn't. I put my head down and walked to my room smiling at everyone I knew. I didn't slow down. I acted as though I had to pee. As though I'd be back in a minute to say good-bye. My ass felt as though I was in the middle of taking a crap, and fuck if I didn't feel blood dripping down my leg.

But fuck it. Maybe I was rushing because I had my period.

Right?

I got into my room and snapped the bathroom door closed behind me. *Do not motherfucking cry, or you're not getting out of here.*

I had to breathe. Just breathe.

Warren had pulled out of my ass and slapped my butt cheek. He'd said, "Thanks, Fiona," as if I'd only told him "no" a hundred times to fulfill his little rape fantasy.

"Fuck off, Warren."

"Aw, come on." He'd tucked his dick back into his pants. "You're being a poor sport."

I'd been kneeling at that point, my pants still around my ankles, and the front of my shirt was covered in leaves and dirt. When I'd looked at him, I thought about what I would do to him when we were both out. I smiled.

The color drained from his face.

As I got in the shower I held that in my memory, nothing else. Cleaning myself. Soap. Washcloth. Drained face. Wiping, scrubbing.

Don't think about it.

My busted ass, the pain inside and out. The pressure marks on my neck. I could think about all that. I could feel all of it.

But my vulnerability? My mortality? My pathetic, helpless whimpers? I wouldn't think about those until I walked out the door.

I got dressed, wincing as I lifted a leg into my pants. No. No wincing. No pain. No outward manifestation of what just happened.

I didn't know what I planned to do about Warren, but I was in control of that. I wouldn't let the emotions of the moment dictate my plan.

"Hey," Jonathan called as I walked down the hall.

"I was looking for you," I said.

"Warren told me."

I swallowed. I was edgy, raw, and a touch away from breaking down, but if I told Jonathan, he'd beat the shit out of the motherfucking psycho-rapist. Then Jon would be stuck in Westonwood, and Warren would get pity. That wouldn't do at all.

"Good," I said. "Margie's picking me up. Wanna come say hi?"

"Nah. I gotta run." He looked me up and down. "You all right?"

"I'm fine."

"You sure? I saw Warren come out of the trees right before you."

"I have to go." When I went to hug him, he grabbed my jaw. I pushed him away. "What's your deal?"

"There are red marks on your neck."

"It's nothing. God, it was grungy behind my ears. I probably just scrubbed too hard."

He didn't believe me. It was all over his face. He held up his hand. "I'm opening pledge."

"No, you don't." I slapped down his hand. If he asked me one more time, I would tell him about not just Warren but Rachel, and we would both go into a tailspin. No, just no. I needed to stay together for five fucking minutes. I didn't want to collapse.

"I don't like that guy," he growled. "He keeps bringing up Dad like it's a joke."

"Ignore him."

"I'm going to punch him."

"Don't, Jon. You were right." I took him by the shoulders. He was so tall, so much a man with his shaved whiskers and lines of rage. "Bite it back. Don't do anything that puts you in a situation where you're not in control. Do you hear me?"

In his green eyes, something flickered, a recognition of the truth, an openness to me I'd never had from him before.

"Are you hearing me?" I said.

"I'm not going to make it."

"You are. You have to. Lock it down. Think. Plan. Will you? Will you be everything I fail at being?"

"You're crazy, you know that?" The crack in his voice belied his words.

I hugged him so hard I thought we'd never separate.

***

I sat at the conference table as if my ass didn't hurt. I concentrated on each breath and just getting the fuck out of there. Margie looked over the papers. Deeming them acceptable, she passed them to me to sign.

"This one verifies you have no complaints against Westonwood you'd like to file," she said.

I signed it.

"This one," Marge said, "is a non-disclosure agreement. You won't disclose their treatment methods or names of any of the patients you met in here."

I signed.

Frances passed her new papers. Margie looked them over, sometimes said this or that, and passed them to me, pointing to the little highlighted ticks indicating where I should scrawl my name. I smiled through the whole thing, even though it was killing me.

"I'll bring the car around," Margie said when it was done.

I counted six couches in the lobby, but I didn't sit on any of them. I had no idea what I would do after Margie pulled around, but I would be out. I would keep everything under control.

Frances hustled through the glass doors. "Fiona."

"Yes?"

She handed me a clipboard. "I forgot this release."

"Oh, okay." I looked for my place to sign, but everything looked hazy.

"Are you all right?" she asked, pointing at the line at the bottom.

"Excited to get going." I signed.

"Have a good trip home, Fiona."

"Thanks."

She was gone in a moment. I glanced at the door. Elliot, a silhouette in the afternoon backlight, opened it and stepped into the building. My heart stopped.

I could have him. With a little effort on my part, and a lot of patience, I could be that perfect, monogamous, plain Jane. I could change my life completely. I pressed my lips together when he stepped toward me. I could be his.

But I couldn't.

How could I do that to him? I was a whore. I was the girl who gave up her ass for a few pills. Even though I knew in my mind it hadn't been my fault and Warren was a piece of shit, another part of me begged to differ. I was a worthless piece of fuckmeat, and even if I kept a lid on my desires for the rest of my life, the fact that my heart was made of cunt wouldn't change.

"Hi," I said.

"Hi," he said. "I was just around, and do you need a lift home?"

He hadn't shaved, and he looked somehow wild and out of sorts. He was so good, so real, a chance at a different life than I'd been prepared for.

"I'm good. But thanks." I couldn't stand there another second. I walked to the door, steeling myself against looking back at him.

As I approached the doors, I felt him behind me. His hand went over mine as it gripped the bar. Margie's BMW was coming around the corner of the drive. I had to just make that difference in distance.

"Fiona, listen," he whispered.

"I can't, Elliot. I can't. I'll destroy you. It's not right." I pushed the door open.

Margie pulled up as if she'd timed it so I wouldn't have to wait more than a second. As I stepped across the concrete toward her, I saw something twenty feet to the right that wasn't visible from the door. A black Range Rover, and a man in a charcoal jacket standing next to it.

Deacon.

It all became clear to me then. I had everything in the world I needed right with him, and he'd come for me as promised, as he always did. He protected me, loved me, worked with who I was instead of trying to transform me into something I'd never be.

I waved at Margie and walked past her. I knew Elliot was behind me, and I knew he saw me approach the Range Rover.

"Master," I said, casting my eyes down.

"My girl."

"May I come with you?"

"There are going to be rules. Do you understand?"

"Yes, Sir."

"And consequences. This can't happen again."

"I understand."

He took me by the chin. "Look at me, kitten."

I did and felt safe. Deacon wouldn't let anything happen to me.

"Who do you see?" he asked.

"My master."

"I have you, darling." He gripped my chin tightly. "I have you."

As I got into the car, I saw Elliot in front of the building with his hands in his pockets. He and Deacon exchanged a stare as my master crossed in front of the car. I closed my eyes and leaned my head back.

I was free, and enslaved, and in control.

I had this.

This ends sequence one...

------

use.

This is as close to a Happy For Now as you're going to get with Fiona. To find out when the next book in *Songs of Perdition is* coming out, get on the mailing list at cdreiss.com

I am going to put out the second book in Antonio and Theresa's story next.

It's titled RUIN.

Expect it in the Fall of 2014. You can add it on Goodreads. Please note, *Songs of Corruption* might go serial. If it does, the next book will be in September. If it stays a full-length trilogy, expect book two in early December. I'll let you know.

Have you read the *Songs of Submission*?

Gracious me. Because fast forward sixteen years and Fiona's brother, Jonathan has this whole thing happening with Monica, a singer with a short-circuiting mouth, and it's all kinds of epic length.

This series was structured like a serial TV show. Novellas were released every four to six weeks, with a break between sequences. Each novella episode was between 20 and 50 thousand words, and ended with unanswered questions.

Sequence 1
Beg
Tease
Submit

Sequence 2
Control
Burn
Resist

Sequence 3
Sing

The Songs of Dominance – ebook only
Jessica/Sharon (to be read after *Submit*)
Rachel (to be read after *Burn*)
Monica (to be read after *Sing)*

How about *Songs of Corruption*? Have you read that?

No?

Well, because when Jonathan says his sister Theresa is going to explode in a firestorm of pearls and lace, he wasn't kidding.

Check out book one, <u>Spin</u>. It's a full length novel.

Made in the USA
Charleston, SC
21 November 2014